"You go without me," she said.

Owen looked at her as if she'd lost her mind. "I am not leaving you," he growled.

The sudden urge to wrap her arms around his neck and kiss him caught her off guard. She'd set aside those nascent feelings of attraction to Owen a long time ago, valuing his loyal friendship far more than she valued any sort of sexual attraction she might feel toward him. To have it come back now, in this awful situation, was confounding.

"Now!" Owen growled, and he tugged her with him through the underbrush to their next bit of cover.

So far, she and Owen seemed to be staying ahead of the danger rustling around in the woods behind them.

But what would happen if they ran out of woods?

FUGITIVE BRIDE

—

PAULA GRAVES

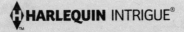

For Melissa, whose cheerleading got me to the end of this book.

Recycling programs
for this product may
not exist in your area.

ISBN-13: 978-0-373-75665-0

Fugitive Bride

Copyright © 2017 by Paula Graves

Printed in U.S.A.

HARLEQUIN®
www.Harlequin.com

Paula Graves, an Alabama native, wrote her first book at the age of six. A voracious reader, Paula loves books that pair tantalizing mystery with compelling romance. When she's not reading or writing, she works as a creative director for a Birmingham advertising agency and spends time with her family and friends. Paula invites readers to visit her website, paulagraves.com.

Books by Paula Graves

Harlequin Intrigue

Campbell Cove Academy

Kentucky Confidential
The Girl Who Cried Murder
Fugitive Bride

The Gates: Most Wanted

Smoky Mountain Setup
Blue Ridge Ricochet
Stranger in Cold Creek

The Gates

Dead Man's Curve
Crybaby Falls
Boneyard Ridge
Deception Lake
Killshadow Road
Two Souls Hollow

Visit the Author Profile page at Harlequin.com for more titles.

CAST OF CHARACTERS

Tara Bentley—Kidnapped on her wedding day, she escapes with the help of her best friend, but they're forced on the run when they learn she's the prime suspect in the murder of the groom.

Owen Stiles—In love with his best friend, who's now a suspect in a murder, the Campbell Cove Academy computer expert will do anything to keep her safe and prove her innocence.

Robert Mallory—He's murdered on his wedding day. But who has a motive?

Archer Trask—The deputy sheriff is in charge of the Mallory homicide case. But will his investigation lead him to a surprising suspect?

Alexander Quinn—Owen's boss at Campbell Cove Academy is willing to break a lot of rules to help Tara and Owen outrun their pursuers. But does he have an ulterior motive?

Maddox Heller—Another of Owen's bosses. Having worked with Archer Trask on a previous case, he hopes he can convince the deputy that Owen and Tara are being framed.

Virgil Trask—Archer Trask's brother, also a Bagley County sheriff's deputy, looks just like one of the men who kidnapped Tara, but is she accusing the wrong man?

Chapter One

The afternoon was perfect for a wedding, currently sunny and mild, with no hint of rain in the forecast until after the ceremony. Staring out the bride's room window at the blooming dogwood trees that lined the church lawn, Tara Bentley had the urge to check her to-do list to see if "achieve a perfect day" was somewhere on the page.

Everything she had so meticulously planned had fallen into place with ease. Her dress fit perfectly. The white tulip bouquet brought out the delicate floral pattern of the lace in her veil. Her wavy hair had, for once, cooperated when the hairdresser straightened it and twisted it into a sleek chignon low at the back of her head, where the snowy veil provided a striking contrast. And she was ten minutes ahead of schedule, which gave Tara a few moments to simply breathe and think about what came next.

Robert. He came next. Robert James Mallory III, successful lawyer and all-around Mr. Perfect. Literally.

Two years ago, as her midtwenties suddenly became her almost-thirties, Tara had written out her list of perfect traits for a potential mate. It hadn't been a particularly long list—she might be hyperorganized and prone to overpreparing, but she wasn't a robot. People weren't ever really perfect, so her list included only things that would be deal breakers.

Things like honesty. Hard work. Respect for her mind. Ambition. And, okay, a few bonus wishes, like a man who was good-looking, fit and amusing.

Three dates with Robert Mallory, and Tara knew she'd met the man who ticked off every item on her checklist. Now she was less than an hour from marrying him.

"I'm so happy," she told the green-eyed woman who stared back at her in the full-length mirror by the vanity table.

Her reflection looked skeptical.

Dang it.

She turned away from the mirror and sat on the small vanity bench, taking care not to wrinkle her wedding dress. Without planning it, she snaked out her hand and snagged the cell phone lying next to her makeup bag. She gave the lock screen a quick swipe and hit the first number on her speed dial.

A familiar, growly voice answered on the second ring, his soft drawl as warm as a fuzzy blanket on a cold Kentucky night. "Shouldn't you be practicing your vows?"

"Owen, am I making a mistake?"

Owen Stiles was quiet for a second. When he spoke again, the lightness of his earlier tone had disappeared. "What's happened?"

The serious tone of his voice made her stomach hurt. What was she doing, dragging poor Owen into her self-doubts? As if he hadn't already suffered half a lifetime of being her sounding board and shoulder to cry on.

"Nothing. Forget I said anything. See you soon." She ended the call and set the phone on the vanity table again.

A few seconds later, the phone trilled, sliding sideways on the table with the vibration. Tara didn't even look at the display. She knew who it was. She picked up the phone. "Owen, I told you it's nothing."

"If you're wondering if you made a mistake, it's not nothing. Are you in the bride's room?"

"Owen—"

His rumbly voice deepened. "I'll be there in two minutes."

"Owen, don't." Her voice rose in frustration.

"Please. Just stay where you are. Everything is fine."

There was a long pause before he spoke again. "Are you sure?"

"Positive. Today is absolutely perfect. Beautiful weather, the sanctuary is gorgeous, my dress fits perfectly and I'm marrying the most perfect man in the world. Nothing can possibly be wrong on a day like this." She stared at the bride in the vanity-table mirror, defiance glaring from her green eyes.

"If you're sure." Owen didn't sound convinced.

"I'll see you at the altar." She hung up the phone again and set it in front of her, her hand flattened against the display.

"Nothing will go wrong," she said to the woman in the mirror.

The bride stared back at her, unconvinced.

It was just cold feet. Everybody got cold feet, right?

This was where having a mom around would have come in handy. Orphanhood sucked. Her mom had died when she was small, and her father had never remarried before his death three years ago. Not that Dale Bentley would have been much help on a day like today. "Suck it up, soldier," she muttered aloud, mimicking her father's gravelly growl. "Make a decision and stick to it."

Man, she missed the old sergeant. He'd have known what to make of Robert. He'd have known whether or not Tara really loved the man or if she loved the idea of him instead.

That was the sticking point, wasn't it? She just wasn't sure she loved the man she was less than an hour away from marrying.

She pushed to her feet. What in the world was she doing getting married if she wasn't sure she loved the man? Had she lost her mind? Was she so addicted to her stupid lists that she trusted them over her own heart?

She had to tell Robert what she was feeling. Talk to him, let him try to talk her out of it. Then she'd know, wouldn't she?

You already know, Tara. Listen to your gut.

Maybe she already knew, but either way, she had to tell Robert. And now, before it was too late.

She was halfway to the door when a knock sounded from the other side. She crossed to the door and leaned her ear close. "Yes?"

The voice from the other side was male and unfamiliar. "Ms. Bentley? There's a package outside we need you to sign for."

"A package?" Sent here, to the church? That was strange. "I'm not expecting anything."

"I don't know, ma'am. It's just for you and it requires a signature. You want me to tell them to send it back?"

"No," she said quickly, curiosity overcoming her impatience. Maybe a distraction was just what she needed to get her head out of her navel for a few minutes. Robert would still be on the other end of the church with his groomsmen, so it wasn't like he'd accidentally get a peek at her dress before the wedding, right?

Assuming there was even going to be a wedding…

Stop it. Just go see what the package is. One thing at a time.

She opened the door to a tall, broad-shouldered man wearing a blue polo shirt and khaki pants. "Hi," she said, feeling a little sheepish as he took in her seed pearl–studded dress and tulle veil. "It's my wedding day."

"I see that." He nodded toward the door down the hall that led to the church's parking lot. "Out here."

She followed him down the hall and out the door, taking care as she crossed the threshold not to let the skirt of her dress get caught in the door closing behind her. Once her dress cleared the door, she started to turn her attention back to the deliveryman, but something dropped over her face suddenly, obscuring her view.

Instinctively sucking in a quick breath, she got a lungful of something sweet and cloying. Her lungs seemed to seize up in response, making it hard to take another breath. Fighting panic, she tried to lift her hands to push the offending material off her face. But thick, strong arms roped around her body, holding her arms in place. Her head began to swim, her throat closing off as she struggled for oxygen. She seemed to float into the air, which was impossible. Wasn't it? She wasn't floating. People didn't float.

Somewhere close by, she thought she heard a voice shouting her name. It sounded familiar, but her suddenly fuzzy brain couldn't make sense of what she was hearing. Then she heard a swift thump and the voice went silent.

There was a metallic clank and suddenly she wasn't floating anymore. She landed with a painful thud onto a hard, cold surface, unable to make sense of what was happening to her. The sweet, slightly medicinal smell permeated everything, seeping into her brain as if it were a sponge soaking up all those heady fumes.

Another thud shook the floor beneath her, and something solid and warm settled against her back. She struggled against the encroaching darkness, one lingering part of her acutely aware that something terribly wrong was happening to her. Today was supposed to be her wedding day, even if she'd decided it was a wedding she didn't want.

She should be looking for Robert to tell him what she'd decided. She had to let people know the wedding was off. She had to call the florists to take away the beautiful roses and tulips that festooned the sanctuary. She supposed she could let the reception go on as planned, feed everyone as an apology for her attack of cold feet.

She had too much to do to be sinking deeper and deeper into the darkness now spreading through her fuzzy brain. But within seconds, she could no longer remember what those things were.

Slowly, inexorably, darkness fell.

OWEN STILES WOKE to darkness and movement. He tried to lift his hands to the hard ache at the back of his head, but his arms wouldn't move. He was bound, he realized, animal panic rising in his throat. He forced it down, trying to remember what he'd learned at Campbell Cove Academy.

First, ascertain where you are and what the danger is.

The where was easy enough. He was in the white van that had been parked outside the church when he went looking for Tara.

He hadn't liked the way she'd sounded on the

phone. And if he was brutally honest with himself, there was a part of him that had been nearly giddy with hope that she was going to call off the wedding.

He wasn't proud of feeling that way. His love for Tara was unconditional. Her happiness meant everything to him.

But he couldn't deny that he wanted her to be happy with him, not some blow-dried, Armani-wearing Harvard Law graduate with a chiseled jaw and a cushy job with a top Louisville law firm.

Ignoring her command to stay put, he'd turned the corner of the hallway that led to the bride's room just in time to see a wedge of tulle and lace disappear through the exit door about twenty yards away.

Hurrying out after her, he'd been just in time to see a large man throw a pillowcase over Tara's head and haul her into a white panel van parked in front of the door. He'd called her name, shock overcoming good sense, and earned a punch that had knocked him into the side of the van. At least, that was the last thing he could remember.

Okay, so he'd ascertained where he was. And the fact that he was trussed up inside the moving van made the danger fairly clear, although he couldn't see anyone lurking around, ready to knock him out again, so he supposed that was a plus.

The back of the van seemed to be closed off from the driver's cab area by a metal panel. That fact posed a problem—he couldn't see how many people were in the front of the van, so he couldn't be sure exactly what he was up against. However, he had seen only two men wrestling with Tara, and they'd both been big guys. He wasn't sure there was room in the van's cab to accommodate more people.

So there were probably two bad guys to deal with. And thanks to the closed-off cab, he could move around unobserved, which would give him a better chance of working out a way to escape.

He felt warmth behind him. Tara?

With a grimace of pain, he rolled over and peered through the gloom. A bundle of silk, lace and tulle lay on the floor of the van beside him. The pillowcase over her head was still there, and he caught a whiff of a faintly sweet, medicinal odor coming from where she lay.

He wriggled closer, ignoring the pounding ache in his head, until his face lay close to the pillowcase. The odor was much stronger suddenly, giving off fumes that made him feel lightheaded.

Ether, he thought. The pillowcase was soaked with ether.

Those idiots! Ether could be deadly if used without care, and they weren't even monitoring her condition.

He jerked at the bindings that held his arms behind his back to no avail. They'd apparently duct-taped his hands together. They weren't going to come apart easily. But he had to get the pillowcase off Tara's head.

Wriggling closer, he gripped the top of the pillowcase with his teeth. The smell of ether nearly overwhelmed him, but he held his breath and tugged upward. Inch by harrowing inch, he dragged the ether-soaked pillowcase from Tara's head until he finally pulled it free.

He spat the taste of ether out of his mouth. Then, his heart in his throat, he leaned over to make sure Tara was still breathing. A few terrifying seconds passed before he felt her breath on his cheek. Shaking with relief, he pressed a kiss to her forehead. "That's my girl. Stay with me, sweetheart."

As he waited for her to come around, Owen started working on the tape that bound his wrists together. His eyes had finally adjusted to the darkness inside the van, giving him a better look at their immediate surroundings.

The interior of the cargo van was empty except for Owen and Tara. Also, what he'd mistaken for a closed panel between them and the front cab wasn't technically closed. There was a large mesh window in the panel that should have given him a look at the occupants of the cab. But their captors had covered the mesh opening with what looked like cardboard, not only blocking out any light coming through the front windows but also keeping them from hearing whatever conversation might be going on between their captors.

The upside to that, Owen thought, was that their captors probably couldn't hear much of what was going on in the back of the van, either.

He looked around for any sharp edges he could use to tear the tape around his wrists. The covering over the wheel well was bolted to the floor of the van, but the bolts were old and worn, not providing much of a cutting edge. Still, he scooted over to the nearest bolt and gave it a try.

The van must have left Mercerville Highway, he realized a few minutes later when the swaying of the vehicle increased, forcing him to plant his feet on the cargo hold's ridged floor to keep from toppling over with each turn. But he couldn't stop Tara from rolling across the floor. A moment later, her head knocked into his hip with a soft thud.

"Ow," she muttered, her voice thick and slurred.

"Oh, sweetheart, there you are," he said softly,

twisting so that his bound hands could reach the side of her face. He brushed away the grit on her cheek with his fingers. "Tara, can you hear me?"

Her head lifted, her hair and the torn remains of her tulle veil obscuring part of her face. "Owen?"

"Yeah, it's me. Careful," he added when she tried to sit up and nearly fell over.

She managed to steady herself in a sitting position and shoved her hair and the veil away from her face with clumsy hands. They, too, were secured by duct tape, he saw, though her captors had bound her hands in front of her rather than behind her. She seemed to belatedly notice the bindings and stared at her wrists. "What's happening?"

"We've been abducted," he said, though he wasn't sure *abduction* was the right term. Neither of them was exactly rolling in dough, so he didn't imagine they'd been taken for ransom purposes. Tara's fiancé was successful but not what anyone would term wealthy. Not yet, anyway.

So why *had* the men grabbed her?

"That's insane," she muttered, still pawing at her veil, which sat askew on her head. "Why am I so woozy?"

"They put a pillowcase over your head." He waved his hand at the offending piece of material lying against the front of the cargo hold. "I think it was soaked with ether."

"Ether?" Tara finally pulled her veil free and threw it on the floor beside her. The van took another turn, forcing Owen to brace himself against the side of the cargo hold. Tara was unprepared, however, and went sprawling against his side, her nose bumping into his shoulder.

"Ow." She righted herself, rubbing her nose. She finally noticed Owen's bound hands, her eyes widening. "You're tied up, too."

"Think you can get the tape off me? Then I'll return the favor." He twisted around until his back was facing her.

"My fingers aren't working so well," she warned him as she started fumbling with the tape. She wasn't lying; it took a full minute before she was able to find the end of the tape on his bindings and start to slowly unwrap his wrists. But she finally ripped away the last of the tape, making the flesh on his wrists sting.

He stretched his aching arms, grimacing at the pain.

"What time is it?" Tara asked.

He pressed the button on his watch that lit up the dial. "Just a little after four."

"Oh."

He turned to look at Tara. "You were supposed to get married at four."

She nodded. "I was supposed to."

He reached for her, taking her bound hands in his. "We'll get you back there, Tara. We'll get out of this and get to a phone so you can call Robert and tell him what happened. And then we'll get you back to the church and you'll get married just the way you planned—"

"I was going to call it off."

He went still. "What?"

In the low light he couldn't make out much about her features, but the tone of her voice was somewhere between sad and embarrassed. "I was going to call it off. Right before that guy knocked on the door and told me there was a package outside."

"That's how they got you outside to the van?"

"Yeah." She wriggled her bound hands at him. "Get this off me, please?"

He pulled the tape from her wrists, taking care with the last few inches to spare her as much of the sting as possible. When she was free, he rolled up the tape from both of their bindings and shoved it in his pocket. It might come in handy if they could get themselves out of this van alive.

Freed from her restraints, Tara curled into a knot beside him, wrapping her arms around her knees. The puffy skirt of her wedding dress ballooned around her, almost glowing in the low light, making her look like a piece of popcorn.

Owen had the clarity of mind not to speak that thought aloud.

He put his arm around her, trying not to read too much into the way she snuggled closer to him. They were in the middle of an abduction. Of course she was seeking a little comfort from the guy who'd been her best friend since middle school.

"What do they want?"

"I don't know," he admitted. "I don't suppose Robert is secretly a multimillionaire with a hefty trust fund?"

"Not that he's ever told me." She made a soft mewling noise. "I am so woozy. They used ether?"

"That's what it smelled like to me."

She cocked her head toward him. "Exactly how do you know what ether smells like?"

"I took a history of medicine course in college, when I was still considering a medical degree."

"And they let you sniff ether?"

Tara's skeptical tone made him smile. She was sounding more like her old self, which meant the effects of the ether were wearing off. "Not on purpose."

He glanced to the far side of the van's cargo

hold, where he'd thrown the ether-soaked pillow-case. In this confined area, the fumes it emitted might still be affecting them, he realized.

"We need to find a way to wrap up that pillowcase so that we limit the fumes it's putting out in this van," he told Tara. "I wish I had a garbage bag or something."

"Don't suppose you carry one of those around in your back pocket?"

"Not in a rented tux, no," he answered with a grin, feeling a little less grim about their chances of survival now that his smart-ass Tara was back. He shrugged off his jacket. "I can wrap it in this."

"The rental place isn't going to like that," Tara warned.

"Not sure it's enough, though."

"Well, I have about twenty yards of silk, lace and tulle you can use." Holding his shoulder, she levered herself to her feet and started to tug at the seams of her skirt until the fabric tore free. In the darkness of the van's enclosed interior, Owen couldn't make out much besides a cloud of faint brightness in the gloom floating away from her body. Tara gathered the fabric into a ball and presented it to him. "Will this do?"

He crossed carefully to the corner of the cargo hold, feeling a distinct unsteadiness he attributed to the moving van, although he should be a lot more worried about the blow he'd taken to the head. He'd been unconscious long enough for their captors to shove him inside the van and tie him up. He might have a concussion. Or worse.

But for now, he was conscious. His head didn't hurt too badly. And he had a job to do.

He wrapped up the pillowcase inside the layers of silk, tulle and lace, and pushed it back into the corner. Already, the distinctively sweet scent of the ether was almost gone.

Gingerly, he edged his way back to where Tara perched on the wheel well cover. "That should take care of—"

The van gave a hard lurch, sending him toppling over. He landed hard on his side, pain shooting through his rib cage and hip.

"Owen!" Tara grabbed his arms and helped him to a sitting position. "Are you all right?"

He rubbed his side, reassuring himself that nothing was broken. "I'm okay—" He broke off, aware that something had changed suddenly.

The engine. He no longer heard the engine noise, or felt the vibration beneath them.

The van had come to a stop.

Chapter Two

Most of the haziness left in her brain from the ether disappeared in a snap when Tara heard the van's engine shut off.

"We've stopped." She looked up at Owen, wishing he wasn't just a shadowy silhouette in the gloom. Sometimes just the sight of him, so controlled and serious, could make her feel as if everything in the world would be okay. At least she could hear his voice, that low Kentucky drawl that had always steadied her like a rock, even in the midst of the craziness life had a habit of throwing her way. "What are they going to do to us now?"

"I don't know. Maybe nothing." He didn't sound confident.

She reached across the narrow space between them and grabbed his hands. "We need a plan."

"We don't have anything to fight with, Tara."

"Yes, we do." She squeezed his hands and

pushed to her feet, heading for the corner where he'd buried the pillowcase inside the remains of her skirt. She grabbed the whole bundle and brought it to where Owen waited.

She saw the faintest glimmer in his eyes when he looked at her, just a hint of light in the darkness. "You are brilliant, sweetheart."

"There were two of them. One who came to get me, telling me there was a package waiting for me, and one standing by the van. I think he was the one who put the pillowcase over my head." She kept her voice low, in case their voices carried outside the van. "They think we're still tied up. At least, we'd better hope they do."

"It'll still take two of them to get us out, so we won't have an advantage. Except surprise."

She grabbed his hand and gave it a squeeze. "Surprise can go a long way. So, first one through the door gets the ether pillowcase over his head."

"And we shove him back onto the second guy while he's off guard."

She looked at Owen, wishing she could see him more clearly. "Think this has a chance of working?"

"No clue, but it's all we've got. So let's make it work." He reached across and gripped her hands briefly. Then he unwrapped the pillowcase from the dress skirt.

The sickly sweet odor of the ether made Tara's stomach twist, but with a little effort she controlled her nerves. She had one job—to fight with every ounce of strength and will she had to get out of this dangerous spot.

At least she wasn't alone. Owen was with her, and if there was one thing in her life she knew completely, it was that Owen would do everything he could to keep her safe. He'd been doing that for her since high school.

The back door of the van rattled, and Tara's heart skipped a beat. She sneaked a quick look at Owen and found him staring at the door, his focus complete.

He'd undergone training at Campbell Cove Academy, which was part of the security company where he now worked, but Tara hadn't really given much thought to what that training entailed. After all, Owen was a computer geek. Computer geeks didn't have much need for ninja skills, did they?

He'd been teased as a child because his skills and talents lent themselves to academic pursuits instead of sports. Even his own father had undermined Owen, calling him weak and inept because he wouldn't try out for the football team in high school.

Tara wished some of those people could see

Owen right now, ready to take on two possibly armed men in order to protect her.

The door to the van opened, and light invaded the back of the van, blinding Tara for a long panicky moment, until a rush of movement from Owen's side of the door spurred her into motion. Her vision adjusted in time for her to see Owen jamming the pillowcase over a man's head and giving him a push backward. The man fell over like a bowling pin, toppling the other man who stood right behind him.

Owen grabbed Tara's hand. "Jump!" he yelled as he jerked her with him out the back door of the van.

She saw the two men on the ground struggling to right themselves. It wouldn't be long before they did, she realized. The thought spurred her to run faster. Thank God she'd opted for low-heeled pumps for her wedding, she thought as she ran across the blacktop road and into the woods on the other side, her hand still firmly clasped in Owen's.

The pumps proved themselves more problematic once they hit the softer ground of the woods. Behind her, the men they'd just escaped started shouting for them to stop, punctuating their calls with a couple of gunshots that made Tara's blood turn to ice. But, as far as she could tell, none of the shots got anywhere near them.

"Come on," Owen urged, pulling her with him as he zigzagged though the woods. It took a couple of minutes to realize there was a method to his seemingly mad dash through the trees. They were moving from tree to tree, finding cover from their pursuers.

What was left of her wedding dress was a liability, she realized with dismay. The white fabric stood out in the dark woods like a beacon. At least Owen's tux was black. He blended into the trees much better than she could hope to do.

"You go without me," she said as they took temporary cover behind the wide trunk of an oak tree. "I'm the one they're after. I stick out like a hooker in a church in this dress. You could find help and send the police after the van. You could tell Robert what happened."

Owen looked at her as if she'd lost her mind. "I am not leaving you," he growled.

The sudden urge to wrap her arms around his neck and kiss him caught her off guard. She'd set aside those nascent feelings of attraction to Owen a long time ago, valuing his loyal friendship far more than she valued any sort of sexual attraction she might feel toward him. To have it come back now, in this awful situation, was confounding.

"Now!" Owen growled, and he tugged her

with him through the underbrush to their next bit of cover.

Behind them, the sound of their pursuers was close enough to spur their forward movement. But the men following them weren't any closer, Tara realized. So far, she and Owen seemed to be staying ahead of the danger pursuing them.

But what would happen if they ran out of woods?

A brisk breeze had picked up as they ran, rustling the leaves overhead. Thank heaven for spring growth; two months ago, these woods would have been winter bare and couldn't have provided them with nearly enough cover. But even here in the Kentucky mountains, the woods couldn't go on forever, which could be a good thing or a bad thing. If they managed to find a well-populated town around the next copse, they'd be safe.

But if they ran into a clearing with neither cover nor the safety of numbers to protect them...

"How long do you think they'll keep chasing us?" she asked breathlessly as they crouched behind another tree.

"I don't know," Owen admitted. "I don't suppose you know why they grabbed you. Did they give you any indication?"

"No, it's like I told you—one of the men came

to get me and the other put the pillowcase over my head before I could even get a good look at his face. Although he definitely asked for me by name. Ms. Bentley." She risked a peek around the side of the tree providing them with cover. "I don't see them anymore."

"I don't think we should move anytime soon. They may be hunkered down, waiting to flush us out."

Tara frowned. "How long are we talking?"

"I don't know. A couple of hours?"

She grimaced. "I suppose it's a bad time to mention that I desperately need to pee."

Owen gave a soft huff of laughter. "Can you hold it awhile?"

"Do I have any choice?"

"No."

"Well, there you go."

Owen gave her a look that made her insides melt a little. She might have decided years ago that she'd rather be his friend forever than risk losing him by taking their relationship to a more sexual place, but that didn't mean she wasn't aware that he found her just as attractive as she found him.

And right now he was looking at her as if he wanted to strip her naked and slake his thirst for her up against the rough trunk of this big oak tree.

Oh, God, Tara, you're hiding from crazy kidnappers and you choose now to conjure up that visual?

"I think I know where we are," Owen murmured a few minutes later.

Moving only her eyes, Tara scanned the woods around them, seeing only trees, trees and more trees. "How on earth is that possible?" she whispered.

"Because while you went to cheerleading camp, I went to Boy Scout camp."

"And what, got a badge in telling one gol dang leafy tree from another?" Staying still was starting to get to her already. She wasn't the kind of woman who stayed still. Ever. And the urge to look behind them to see if their captors were sneaking up on them was almost more than she could bear.

"No," Owen said with more patience than she deserved. "It's because I stayed in a rickety little cabin with five other boys about two hundred yards to our east."

She slanted a look at him. "How can you possibly know that?"

"See that big tree right ahead? The one with the large moon-shaped scar on the trunk about five feet up?"

She peered through the trees. "No."

"Well, trust me, it's there. And that moon

shape is there because Billy Turley and I carved it in the trunk on a dare. Our camp counselor didn't buy that we were trying out our trailblazing skills like Daniel Boone before us."

There had never been a time in her life when she'd felt less like smiling, but the image conjured up by Owen's words made her lips curve despite herself. She and Owen had met around the time they were both in sixth grade. In fact, she could remember Owen taking that trip to the woods because she'd been over-the-moon excited about being invited to cheerleading camp, since only girls who went to the camp in middle school ever made the varsity squad in high school.

Oh, for the days when life was so simple that her biggest worry was crash-landing a herkie jump in front of twenty other judgmental preteen girls.

"I know you're about ready to squirm out of your skin," Owen said quietly, slipping his hand into hers, "but I have a plan."

She curled her fingers around his. "Okay. What is it?"

"As soon as I'm pretty sure our kidnappers have retreated, we'll head for the cabin."

She looked up at him, narrowing her eyes. "The one you stayed in twenty years ago when you were eleven?"

"I think it's still there."

"Maybe, but in what kind of condition?"

His lips flattened with exasperation. She felt his grip on her hand loosen. "Must you always be so negative?"

She tightened her fingers around his again. "Yes. But sorry."

He gave her fingers a light squeeze. "I suppose it's part of your charm."

"Sweet talker," she muttered.

"So we're agreed? We head for the cabin?"

"If it's still there." She looked up. "Sorry. Negativity."

"If it's still there," he agreed. "And we'd better hope it is."

The dark tone of his growly voice made her stomach turn a flip. "Why's that?"

"You know how the wind has picked up?"

"Yeah?"

"I think the rain may be getting here a little earlier than expected tonight."

Owen was right. Within a few minutes, the brisk wind began to carry needles of rain from which the spring growth overhead provided only partial shelter. Owen tried to tuck Tara under his coat, but the rain became relentless as daylight waned, darkness falling prematurely because of the lowering sky.

Tara wiped the beading water from her watch

face. Nearly six. The wedding would have long been over by now, if she'd gone through with it. Robert must be going crazy, wondering what happened to her. Her car would still be in the parking lot, her purse in the bride's room. The only thing missing was the bride and her puffy white dress.

Would everyone realize something had gone very wrong? Or would they assume that Tara had succumbed to cold feet and bolted without letting anyone know?

Was Robert thinking he'd just made a narrow escape from a lifetime with a lunatic?

Stop it, Tara. This is not your fault.

Owen was right. She was way too negative. She added it to her mental list of things she needed to work on, right behind cellulite on her thighs and—oh, yeah—running away from dangerous, crazy kidnappers.

"You're thinking, aren't you?" Owen asked. "I always worry when you're thinking."

"I'm thinking I haven't heard anything from the kidnappers back there recently. I'm also thinking that there may be ants crawling up my legs. And I'm thinking if I have to hide behind this tree for a minute longer, getting soaked to the skin, I'm going to run crazy through the trees, screaming *I give up! Come get me!* at the top of my lungs."

Owen turned toward her, cupping her face between his hands. His fingers were cool, but the look in his eyes was scalding hot. "I know you're scared. I know wisecracking and complaining is how you show it. And you're right. We haven't heard those guys recently. I don't think they were eager to spend the rest of their day hunting you down in the woods when they know who you are and can take a chance on grabbing you another time."

She stared up at him. "You really think they'll try this again?"

"You said they asked for you by name."

"But why? I'm not rich. Robert's not even rich, not really. Not enough to warrant a risky daylight abduction."

"I know. But even if you can't think of a reason, they clearly had one." He dropped his hands to his sides. "It's time to make a run for it. You ready?"

"Born ready." She flashed him a cheeky grin, even if she felt like crying. It earned her one of Owen's deliciously sexy smiles in return, and he touched her face again. His fingers were cold, but heat seemed to radiate through her from his touch.

He grabbed her hand and started running, pulling her behind him.

Even though she'd convinced herself that

their captors had given up and made their escape, every muscle in Tara's body tensed as she zigzagged behind Owen, her heart in her throat. Every twig that snapped beneath her feet sounded as thunderous as a gunshot, even through the masking hiss of the falling rain.

Two hundred yards to the cabin, Owen had said. Surely they'd run two hundred yards by now. That was two football fields, wasn't it?

Owen jerked sideways suddenly, nearly flinging her off her feet. He grabbed her around the waist as she started to slide across the muddy ground and kept her upright. "There," he said, satisfaction coloring his voice.

Tara followed his gaze and saw what looked to be a ramshackle wooden porch peeking out from the overgrowth about twenty yards away.

"You have got to be kidding me," she muttered.

His lips pressed to a thin line. "Shelter is shelter, Tara." He let go of her hand and started toward the wooden structure with a brisk, determined stride.

She stood watching him for a moment, feeling terrible. The man had saved her life, and she'd been nothing but a whining ingrate.

Lighting flashed overhead, followed quickly by a bone-rattling boom of thunder that shook her out of her misery and sent her dashing through the muddy undergrowth as fast as her ruined pumps would carry her. She skidded to a stop at the edge of the porch and stared at what Owen had called a cabin.

It was tiny. She didn't have any idea how Owen and his fellow Boy Scouts had managed to squeeze themselves inside the place. The three shallow steps leading up to the porch looked rickety and dangerous, though apparently they'd managed to hold Owen's weight, for he was already on the porch, peering inside the darkened doorway of the small structure.

"I remember it as being bigger," he said quietly.

"You were eleven." She made herself risk the steps. They were sturdier than they looked, though the rain had left them slick. At least the stair railing didn't wiggle too much as she climbed to the porch and joined Owen in the doorway.

Years had clearly passed since any Boy Scouts had darkened the door of this cabin. What she could see in the gloom looked damp and dilapidated. The musty smell of age and disuse filled Tara's lungs as she took a shaky breath. "The roof leaks, doesn't it?"

Owen took a step inside. Almost immediately, he jerked back, bumping into Tara. She had to grab him around the waist to keep from falling.

Something small and gray scuttled out the door past them, scampered off the porch and disappeared into the undergrowth.

"Possum," Owen said.

Tara grimaced. "So that's what I'm smelling."

He whipped around to look at her. "I'm sorry I've disappointed you. Again."

She grabbed his hand. "You saved me. I wouldn't have gotten out of there without you."

He gave her hand a little squeeze before letting go. "If it weren't for you, I'd have never gotten loose from that duct tape."

And he'd never have been in trouble if she hadn't called him to share her doubts about the wedding. Which maybe she wouldn't be having if she didn't still find Owen so darn attractive.

They could play this game forever, going all the way back to sixth grade when she saved Owen from a bully and he'd helped her pass math.

They were darn near symbiotic at this point.

"You're thinking again," Owen murmured.

"I am," she said. "I'm thinking if we're planning on hunkering down here until the rain passes, I'd like to make sure there's no possum surprises waiting for me in there. Any chance we could find a candle or two in this godforsaken place?"

"Maybe." Owen entered the dark cabin. A moment later, she heard more than saw him scrabbling around in a drawer. "Ha." He reached into the pocket of his tuxedo pants and pulled out something. A second later, a small light flickered in the darkness.

"You had a lighter in your pants pocket?"

"I wanted to be sure your candle lighting at the wedding went off without a hitch." He shot her a sheepish grin. "I take my man-of-honor duties seriously."

Her insides melted, and she crossed to where he stood, wrapping her arms around his waist and pressing her face to his chest. "You're the best man of honor ever."

He rubbed his free hand down her arm. "Oh, Tara, you're freezing. You really need to get out of those wet clothes."

"And into what?" she asked, her voice coming out softer and sultrier than she'd intended.

He stared back at her, wordless, his eyes smoldering as strongly as the flickering candle in his hand. The moment stretched between them, electric and fraught with danger.

And forbidden desires…

A loud thud sounded outside the door, and in a flash, Owen extinguished the candle and pulled Tara behind him.

There was another thud. Slow. Deliberate.

Someone was outside the cabin.

Chapter Three

Owen tucked Tara more fully behind him, squaring his shoulders in an attempt to look larger than he was. What he wouldn't give to have the pecs and deltoids of Mike Strong, who'd instructed him in hand-to-hand combat during his first grueling weeks of probationary training at Campbell Cove Security Services. Strong had insisted that Owen's lean, wiry build didn't mean he couldn't hold his own in a fight, but until today, he'd never had a reason to test that theory.

And given how badly his attempt to save Tara outside the church had gone, he wasn't confident that Strong would be proven right this time, either.

He could hear his father's voice, a mean whisper in his ear. "You're weak, Owen. Life ain't kind to the weak."

Grimly shutting out that voice, he searched the shadowy interior of the cabin for something he could use as a weapon, but the place had been stripped mostly bare a long time ago, from the looks of it. There was a rickety camp bed left in one corner, and the mattress of another lying on the floor nearby, but that was all. What he wouldn't give for one of those cheap little bow and arrow sets he and the other Scouts had learned to use that summer twenty years ago.

Not that he'd remember how to use it.

The footsteps on the porch moved closer, the steps careful. Deliberate. There was an oddly light touch to the sounds that didn't remind him much of the hulking men who'd shoved him into the side of the van earlier that day. These foot-falls sounded almost—

A face peered around the edge of the door. Small, pale, freckled and terrified.

A kid, no more than ten or eleven. He froze there, his face framed by the bright red hood of his rain slicker. A second later, a second face appeared next to the boy's, smaller. More feminine. She had big, dark eyes and frizzy curls framing her face beneath her pink rain hood.

Owen took a step toward them. "Hello—"

The boy opened his mouth and screamed, triggering an answering shriek in the girl. They sped off into the rainy woods, their terrified wails turning to hysterical giggles of pure adrenaline rush before they faded from earshot.

Owen felt Tara's forehead press hard against his back. "Kids?"

"That could have been us twenty years ago." Owen turned to look at her. "Sneaking around Old Man Ridley's cabin, trying to catch him red-handed at murder."

Tension seeped slowly out of her expression, a faint smile taking its place. "Remember that summer he almost caught us?"

"One of the top ten most terrifying moments of my life." He laughed softly.

"Do you think those kids will come back with grown-ups next time?"

He shook his head. "Are you kidding? They'd probably be grounded for life just for sneaking around this old cabin." He pulled out the lighter and relit the candle he'd extinguished. "Come on, let's see what kind of shelter we can make of this place."

The place was grimy and drafty, but the tin roof seemed to have weathered the years without springing leaks, which had kept the interior dry and mostly free of mildew. The cot mattresses were a disaster, but Owen uncovered an old military footlocker half hidden by the remains of one of the cots. Inside, he found a couple of camp blankets kept well preserved within the airtight trunk. They smelled of the cedar blocks someone had placed inside the trunk to ward off moths.

"Here, wrap up in this." He unfolded the top blanket and wrapped it around Tara's shoulders, not missing the shivers rattling through her. "I wish we could risk starting a fire in that fireplace," he said with a nod toward the river stone fireplace against the near wall. "But the chimney's probably blocked by now, and besides, we don't want to risk smoke alerting anyone to where we are. Not yet."

She stepped closer to him, curling into him like a kitten seeking heat. "Just hold me for a minute, okay? They say body heat is the best heat."

Owen quelled the instant reaction of his body to hers, a talent he'd honed since their early teens, when Tara's femininity blossomed in time for his hormones to rev up to high gear. She'd put deliberate boundaries between them, first unspoken ones and then, later, when he'd wanted to push those barriers out of the way, spoken ones.

"I've never had a friend like you, Owen," she'd told him that night after the high school football game when he tried to kiss her in the car after he'd driven her home. "I need you to be Owen. My best friend. We can't risk changing that. Do you understand? Boyfriends are complicated.

Relationships are volatile. I have enough of that in my life."

He couldn't argue with that. Motherless since just before they'd met, Tara had struggled to connect with her rough-edged, emotionally conservative father, who'd had to give up the military life he'd loved to take care of his daughter. Tara had felt as if he resented her for the end of his Marine Corps career, which had added to the existing friction between them right up until his death.

Owen had swallowed his desire and given Tara what she needed, as much as it had cost him to do so. But the desire had never gone away, married as it was to his enduring love for his best friend.

And at times like these, with her slender body pressed so intimately to his, what was left of her clothing clinging to her body and leaving little to his imagination, tamping down that desire was a Herculean task.

"Maybe the rain will stop soon," she mumbled against his collarbone, her breath hot against his neck.

"Maybe," he agreed. "Those children must live nearby, which is promising, because when this was a Boy Scout camp years ago, there were no houses in easy walking distance at all."

She burrowed deeper in his embrace. "I wonder how I'm going to explain walking around in the woods wearing a slip, half a wedding dress and my ruined silk pumps."

"Very carefully," he answered, making her chuckle. The sound rippled through him, sparking a shudder of pure male need.

"I don't think the rain is supposed to end before morning," she said with a soft sigh that heated his throat again. "We're going to need to find somewhere to sleep tonight. And I have to say, I'm not thrilled about sharing a cot where a possum was probably nesting."

"The blankets from that chest are pretty clean. We could cover the mattresses with those."

"Mattress," she corrected.

"Mattress?"

She looked up at him, her expression serious. "It's too cold in here for us to sleep apart. Right?"

He stared at her, his heart rattling in his chest like a snare drum. He swallowed hard and forced the words from his lips. "Right. Body heat is the best heat."

He was in so much trouble.

BAGLEY COUNTY SHERIFF'S DEPARTMENT investigator Archer Trask walked slowly around the small groom's room, taking in all the details of the crime scene. There was less blood than one might expect, to begin with. The victim had taken two bullets to the base of his skull—double tap, the big-city cops would call it. A sign of a professional hit.

But who the hell would target a groom on his wedding day?

"Vic's name is Robert Mallory. The third." The responding deputy flipped a page in his notepad. "Mallory Senior works in the Lexington DA's office, and he's already screaming for us to turn this over to the Kentucky State Police."

"Any witnesses?"

"No, but the bride is missing. So's her man of honor."

Trask slanted a look at the deputy. "You're kidding."

"Nobody's seen either of them since about an hour before the wedding."

"Bride's name?"

"Tara Bentley."

Didn't sound familiar. Neither did the groom's name. "Have you talked to the bride's parents?"

"She's an orphan, it seems." The deputy grimaced. "Her side of the aisle is a little sparse."

Trask rubbed his forehead, where a headache was starting to form. Why didn't he ever get a cut-and-dried case these days? "I want the groom's parents kept apart so I can question them separately. And any of the wedding party who might have seen anything. Do we have an estimated time of death yet?"

"Last time anyone saw him was around three, about an hour before the ceremony was supposed to start. Last time anyone saw the bride was round the same time."

Trask frowned. Missing bride, dead groom, professional-looking hit—nothing seemed to fit. "You said man of honor."

The deputy flipped back a page or two in his notepad. "Owen Stiles. Apparently the bride's best friend from childhood."

Stiles. The name sounded familiar. "What do we know about Stiles?"

"Not much. His mother is here for the wedding. She's the one who told us she couldn't find him. By the way, according to the man of honor's mother, their cars are still in the church parking lot."

Trask looked up at the deputy's words. "You're telling me the bride and her best friend took a flyer and left their cars behind?"

"Looks like. We've already checked the tags and they're registered to our missing persons."

Well, now, Archer thought. That was a surprising twist. "Let's get an APB out on both of them. Persons of interest in a murder for now.

We need to check if either of them have another vehicle, too."

"I'll call it in." The deputy finished jotting notes and headed out of the room.

Trask looked down at the dead man lying facedown on the floor. Poor bastard, he thought. All dressed up and nowhere to go.

"Do you, Tara, take Robert as your lawfully wedded husband? To have and to hold from this day forward. For better or worse, in sickness and in health, forsaking all others..." The pastor's intonation rang in Tara's head, making it throb. She wanted to run, but her feet were stuck to the floor as if her shoes were nailed to it. She tried to tug her feet from the shoes, but they wouldn't budge.

Breathing became difficult behind the veil that had seemed to mold itself around her head and neck, tightening at her throat. She attempted to claw it away, but the more she pulled at the veil, the more it constricted her.

"Owen!" she cried, the sound muffled and puny. She knew he was here somewhere. Owen would never let anything bad happen to her.

"I'm here." His voice was a warm rumble in her ear, but she couldn't see him.

"Owen, please."

Arms wrapped around her from behind.

Owen's arms, strong and bracing. The veil fell away and she could breathe again. Her feet pulled loose from the floor and she turned to face her rescuer.

Owen gazed at her, his face so familiar, so right, even in the shadows.

"You awake now?"

The shadows cleared, and she realized where she was. It was the old Boy Scouts camp cabin in the woods. Night had passed, and with it the rain. Misty sunlight was peeking through the trees outside and slanting into the cabin through the dusty windows.

And she was wrapped up tightly in Owen's arms on the mattress they shared.

"Yes," she answered.

"You were dreaming. Must have been a bad one."

She forced a smile, the frightening remnants of her nightmare lingering. "Just a stress dream. You know, late for class."

"You called out to me."

She eased away from his embrace and sat up. "Probably wanted you to do my algebra homework for me."

He sat up, too. The blanket spilled down to his waist, revealing his lean torso. She rarely saw him shirtless, and it came as a revelation. Owen might not be bulked up like a bodybuilder, but his shoulders were broad, his stomach flat and his chest well-toned. He'd talked often about Campbell Cove Security's training facilities, which were apparently part of the company's connected training academy, but she'd been so wrapped up in her wedding plans she hadn't listened as closely as she should have.

"Did you hear it, too?" he asked in a half whisper, and she realized he'd been talking to her while she was ogling his body.

She lowered her voice to match his. "Hear what?"

"Voices. I think I'm hearing voices outside. Listen."

Tara listened. He was right. The voices were faint, but they were there. "A woman and a man," she whispered. "Can't make out what they're saying."

"Maybe one of those kids did tell their parents about seeing us last night." Owen rose, grabbing his shirt from where it lay on the floor nearby and slipping it on as he crossed to the cabin's front window. Tara noticed that grime had smudged the snowy-white fabric.

"Can you see anyone?" she whispered.

He nodded. "They look normal."

"By normal, I assume you mean nonhomicidal."

He turned to flash her a quick grin. "Exactly."

"Maybe we should go out and meet them. It'll look less suspicious."

"Good idea." He glanced her way. "Wrap the blanket around your bottom half. It'll be hard to explain half a wedding dress."

Smart, she thought, and grabbed the blanket that had been covering them to wrap around her. She joined him at the door. "Ready?"

He took her hand. "Let's not tell them what really happened. Too hard to explain. I'm just going to say we're newlyweds whose car broke down in the storm."

"Okay." She twined her fingers with him and followed him onto the porch, surprising the couple approaching the cabin through the underbrush.

"Oh!" the woman exclaimed as they came to a quick halt. "I reckon y'all are real after all."

"You must be the parents of one of the kids we scared last night," Owen said with an engaging smile. "Sorry about that."

The woman, a plump brunette with a friendly smile, waved off his apology. "Don't you worry about that. Those young 'uns had no business bein' out here in the middle of a rainstorm. But we figured we should at least come out here and make sure you weren't in some kind of trouble."

The man grimaced at the cabin. "Y'all had to sleep here last night?"

"Sadly, yes," Owen said. "Our car broke down late yesterday afternoon, and then the rain hit, so we had to settle for what shelter we could find. And then, to our complete horror, we discovered we'd both left our cell phones at the church. So we couldn't even call for a tow."

The woman took in their appearances—the beaded bodice of Tara's torn dress, Owen's grimy white tuxedo shirt and black pants—and jumped to the obvious conclusion. "You're new-lyweds, aren't you? Bless your hearts—this is where you spent your wedding night?"

Owen laughed, pulling Tara closer. "It'll be quite the story to tell on our golden anniversary, won't it? I don't suppose we could borrow a phone to call for help?"

"Of course you could." The woman dug in the pocket of her jeans and provided a cell phone. "Here you go."

"Thank you so much." Owen took the phone and went back inside the cabin to make the call, leaving Tara to talk to the friendly couple.

"Do you live close?" Tara asked.

"Half a mile. Kind of hard to see the place through all the trees. If it was winter, you'd probably have seen us and not had to spend the night here," the husband said. "I'm Frank Tyler, by the way. This is my wife, Elaine."

"Tara B—Stiles. Tara Stiles, and my husband's name is Owen." Tara smiled, even though her stomach was starting to ache from the tension of lying to this nice couple. But Owen was right. As crazy as the "newlyweds with car trouble" story was, the truth was so much more problematic.

Owen came back out to the porch, a smile pasted on his face. But Tara knew him well enough to know that his smile was covering deep anxiety. It glittered in his eyes, tense and jittery. He handed the phone back to Elaine Tyler. "Thank you so much. I've called someone for a tow, so we're set."

"Glad we could help. You know, we could drive you to where your car is parked."

"Not necessary. I've arranged for someone to meet us on Old Camp Road. Easy walk from here to there. You should get back to your family." Owen shook Frank Tyler's hand, then Elaine's. "Thank you again."

"Yes, thank you so much," Tara added, smiling brightly to hide her growing worry. Who had Owen called and what had he heard?

When the Tylers were out of earshot, Tara moved closer to Owen. "What's wrong?"

He caught her hand, his expression pained.

"Tara, I don't know how to break this to you. Robert's dead."

She stared at Owen, not comprehending. "What?"

"He's dead. Shot, from what my boss told me."

She covered her mouth with one shaky hand, not certain what she was feeling. Her fiancé was dead. The man she'd been close to marrying. Even if she had become convinced he wasn't the man for her, it didn't mean she hadn't cared deeply for him.

And now he was gone? Just like that?

It was crazy. It had to be wrong.

"This has to be a mistake," she said, her legs suddenly feeling like jelly.

Owen led her to the steps and eased her into a sitting position on the top step. Ignoring the uncomfortable dampness of the wood, she turned to look at Owen as he settled down beside her and wrapped one strong arm around her shoulder. "I'm so sorry, sweetheart."

She leaned her head against his shoulder. "There's more, isn't there?"

He leaned his head against hers. "Yes."

She sighed. "Just get it over with."

"Robert was murdered at the church around the time you and I were taken by the kidnappers. Nobody knew where we went, so—"

"So now we're the prime suspects," she finished for him.

Chapter Four

"How long do you think it'll take your boss to get here?"

Owen looked away from the empty road, taking in the lines of tension in Tara's weary face. "He should be here soon. It's not that far from the office to here."

He didn't know how to comfort her when his own nerves were stretched to the breaking point. How had they gone from kidnap victims to murder suspects in the span of a few hours? And how could they ever prove their story? The only evidence left was a wad of duct tape still hidden in his tux pants, which was hardly dispositive. Any ether left in Tara's system would be long gone by now, and any ether that might have been deposited on her hair and clothing would have been washed away by the rain.

"What are we going to do, Owen?" Tara looked tiny, wrapped up as she was in the drab camp blanket. "What did your boss say we should do? Turn ourselves in?"

"He just told me to sit tight and let him figure it out." Owen didn't like admitting that he didn't have a clue what they should do, either, but he'd never been a suspect in a murder before.

"Do you trust him?"

How to answer that question? Owen technically had three bosses—Alexander Quinn, Rebecca Cameron and Maddox Heller, the three former government employees who now ran Campbell Cove Security Services. Cameron, a former diplomat, and Heller, a former marine, seemed nice enough, but Owen's department, Cybersecurity, was mainly under the hawkeyed control of Quinn, a former spy with an epic reputation for getting things done no matter the cost.

Owen didn't know if it was ever wise to trust someone like Quinn, who saw even his employees as expendable if it meant securing the safety of the country he'd spent decades serving. But Owen had no doubt that Quinn was dedicated to the cause of justice. And if he and Tara ended up in jail for something they didn't do, how would justice be served?

"I think he'll want the right person to go to jail for what happened to Robert," he said finally.

Tara's narrow-eyed gaze told him she hadn't been mollified by his answer. "Well, he'd better get here soon, because it won't take long for those nice people we met this morning to find out about Robert's murder on the morning news and start to wonder about that half-dressed bride and groom they saw hiding in the woods."

She was right. Owen checked his watch. Where the hell was Quinn? "I wish I had my phone."

"Is that him?" Tara nodded toward a small, dark dot at the far end of the narrow two-lane road. It grew bigger as it came near, resolving into a dark blue SUV. It stopped about forty yards down the road, and a sandy-haired man got out.

Not Quinn but Maddox Heller. Owen didn't know whether to be worried or relieved.

Heller motioned for them to come to him. Grimacing, Owen started walking. The rain had tightened the leather of his dress shoes, which were pinching his feet. Tara didn't look any happier about the walk, wobbling a little in her grimy pumps and taking care not to step on the hem of her blanket wrap.

"Sorry," Maddox said when they reached the SUV. "I wanted to be sure you weren't being used as bait for an ambush."

Tara pulled herself into the front seat and sighed deeply. "Twenty-four hours ago, my life was so simple."

Heller gave her a sympathetic look. "I'm sorry about your fiancé. Are you warm enough? Let me turn up the heater."

Owen sat on the bench seat behind them, closing his hand over Tara's shoulder. He felt her skin ripple beneath his touch, but when he started to pull his hand away, she caught it and held it in place.

"For now, I'm taking you to a safe house. We'll get you some clothes and something to eat, and you can try to get some sleep. I can't imagine you slept well in a cold cabin."

"What about the police?" Tara asked.

"Quinn wants to look into that issue before we decide what to do. For now, he wants you to just stay put."

Easy enough, Owen thought. He wanted nothing more than a hot meal, some warm, dry clothes and to sleep for a week.

"Do you know how Robert was killed?" Tara asked as Maddox reversed the SUV and headed back the way he'd come. "Owen said he was shot, but when? How?"

"The details are sketchy. We have some friends in the local sheriff's department, but they're hunkered down at the moment, as you can imagine, just dealing with the press and with your fiancé's family."

Tara rubbed her forehead. "I didn't even think

about his poor parents. Who would do something like that? And why?"

Owen squeezed her shoulder. "We're going to find out. I promise."

She looked at him over her shoulder. "You can't promise that."

"I promise to do everything I can to figure this out and keep you safe."

She smiled wanly. "I know you'll try."

The drive to the safe house took about twenty minutes, taking them out of the woods and down a long country road dotted here and there with farms and pastureland where horses grazed placidly in the morning sun. Halfway there, Maddox Heller turned on the radio and tuned in to a local news station, which was covering Robert's murder with almost salacious excitement.

They learned nothing new, however, and Tara bluntly asked Heller to turn it off.

The safe house was a small, neat farmhouse nestled near the end of a two-lane road sheltered on either side by apple trees. There were no other houses on the road, no doubt by design. Even the house itself was sheltered on three sides by sprawling oak trees that hid most of the property from view unless someone was driving by on purpose.

"It's fairly rustic," Heller warned as he led them up the flagstone walkway to the river stone porch. "But you'll have what you need, and the property is protected by a state-of-the-art security system."

"Will there be anyone protecting us?" Tara asked. "I mean, if those guys who grabbed us try to find us again."

Heller glanced at Owen. "Owen's trained for the basics. The security system should do the rest, and we'll have an agent check on you regularly until Quinn decides how to proceed. You shouldn't be here long."

Tara glanced Owen's way. He wasn't sure if she was looking for reassurance or expressing skepticism. He smiled back at her, hoping it would suffice as a response either way.

Heller showed them how to set and disarm the security system. "You can set your own codes if that makes you feel more secure, or you can leave the code as is. We have an override code in case there's trouble, but only Cameron, Quinn and I know that code, so you should be very safe."

He led them deeper into the house. It was rustic, as Heller had warned, but everything looked to be in good working shape. There was wood in the bin next to the fireplace, and the kitchen appliances proved to be up-to-date. "We stocked the fridge and freezer, so you'd have enough to eat for a few days if things don't resolve sooner,"

Heller told them as they left the kitchen and entered the hallway that led to a couple of large bedrooms near the back of the house. He guided Tara to the room on the right. "There are several sizes of clothing you can choose from in there. We took up a collection from all the women we could reach on quick notice. Hopefully, you'll find a few things that work. Let me know if you don't." He nodded toward the other room. "I grabbed some of the stuff you had stashed at work, and got a few of the taller guys to lend you some clothes," he told Owen.

Heller followed Owen into the room and closed the door behind them. "You okay? Quinn said you had a knock on the head. Did you lose consciousness?"

"Briefly," Owen answered. "I'm fine."

"I could have Eric come take a look at you, although Quinn wants to keep as few people as possible in the loop on this, at least until he can get a better idea what's going on."

"I haven't had any symptoms. My head doesn't even hurt where I hit it, except a little tenderness in the skin."

Heller took a look at the lump on the side of Owen's head, frowning. "Don't take chances. Head injuries aren't anything to mess around with."

"I'm fine."

"What about Tara? Any lingering effects from the ether exposure?"

"Not that I can tell. I'll keep an eye on her."

Heller opened the top drawer of the tall chest next to the bedroom door and withdrew a lockbox. He set it on the bed and opened it with a key he pulled from his jeans pocket. Inside, nestled in foam padding fitted snugly to it, lay a Smith & Wesson M&P .380. "There's ammo in the drawer. Quinn said you'd been trained to use one of these."

Owen stared at the pistol, trying not to feel queasy. "I have, but—"

"No buts. You're trained to use it. Which means you also know when not to use it. Trust your training. And your own good sense." Heller handed Owen the key. "Quinn sent over a team from your department to set up a computer. You should be able to access the office server through an untraceable remote access program. I'm told you're the one who created the system, so I'm sure you know how to make it work."

Owen managed a weak smile, his gaze wandering back to the open pistol case. "Computers I can do."

Heller clapped his hand over Owen's shoulder. "You can handle all of it. Remember your training. Let it do the work for you."

Owen walked Heller to the front door. "Any

idea when we can expect to hear something from you or Quinn or whoever?"

"Soon. I can't be more specific until Quinn's finished his investigation." Heller's smile carved dimples in his tanned cheeks, making him look a decade younger. "We're on your side, Stiles. Try to relax. We'll be in touch."

Owen blew out a long breath after he closed the door behind Heller, his heart pounding in his chest. What the hell had he and Tara stumbled into? And how was he supposed to protect her when he was shaking in his boots?

"There's a gun on your bed."

Tara's voice made him jump. He turned to look at her. "Heller left it for me, in case we need it."

Her eyes narrowed. "Do you know how to use it?"

"Yes."

She looked tired and scared, her arms wrapped protectively around herself. Still in the tattered remains of her wedding dress, she looked small and vulnerable, two words he'd never before associated with Tara. The Tara he knew was fierce and invincible. Seeing her so uncertain, so fragile, made his stomach ache.

"You need a shower and some sleep." He crossed to where she stood, rubbing his hands lightly up and down her arms. "Come on, let's see if we can find the bathroom."

She flung her arms around him suddenly, pressing her face to his chest. Her arms tightened around his waist, her grip fierce. "Thank you."

He wrapped his arms around her, wishing he could ease the tremble he felt in her limbs. "For what?"

"You came to find me, even when I told you not to worry." She looked up at him. "You always do."

"Always will," he promised.

Her gaze seemed to be searching his face for something. He wasn't sure what. Reassurance? Reliability?

Tell me what you want, Tara, and I'll give it to you.

"You're right about one thing. I need a shower and about a week of sleep," Tara said, pulling away from his embrace.

He needed a shower, too, but he felt suddenly wide awake, as if the reality of their dilemma had flooded his veins with adrenaline. He needed to figure out why Robert had been murdered and how it related to Tara's kidnapping.

Tara had disappeared into her room, and the sound of running water coming from behind the closed door meant there must be a bathroom connected to her room. His bedroom didn't have an en suite bathroom, but the large bathroom just down the hall was more than convenient.

He took a quick shower, changed into a pair of jeans and a thick sweatshirt, and settled down at the desk nestled in the corner of his bedroom, where one of his colleagues in the computer security section had provided a high-tech setup.

Everything was up and running, so he connected to the Campbell Cove Security system and quickly found the files on Robert Mallory's murder. The details were sketchy, but the agent Quinn had assigned to compile information, Steve Bartlett, had pulled together a timeline of the murder, including the details Owen had provided to Quinn over the phone.

The coroner would narrow down the time of death, but witness testimony suggested that he'd been killed between two thirty, when his father had talked to him briefly as the groom was dressing, and around three thirty, when the best man had stopped in the groom's dressing room for a last minute pep talk and found his body.

Tara had been abducted about ten minutes after three, which gave her only a partial alibi for the murder, unless the coroner could nail down a more precise time of death for Robert. Had her abduction been part of the murder plot?

But why grab her? Why not just shoot her the way Robert had been shot?

Owen rubbed his gritty eyes. Adrenaline might be keeping his brain awake, but his body was aching with exhaustion. He needed rest. To give his brain a break so he'd be focused and clearheaded enough to make sense of the tangled threads that might—or might not—connect the abduction and the murder.

The only thing Owen was sure about was his own involvement. He wouldn't have been anywhere near Tara and her kidnappers if she hadn't made that phone call to him. He had been in the church vestibule with the bridesmaids and would have remained there until Tara arrived for the start of the ceremony.

He had been collateral damage. Tara had been the target.

But why?

"I couldn't sleep."

His keyed-up nerves jumped at the sound of Tara's voice behind him. He swiveled his chair to look at her and felt an immediate jolt to his libido.

Her dark hair, still damp from the shower, fell in tousled waves over her shoulders. She'd found a long-sleeved T-shirt that fit snugly over her curves. It was thin enough for him to see that she wasn't wearing a bra.

He forced his gaze down to the slim fit of the gray yoga pants that revealed the rest of her curves, the well-toned thighs and shapely calves. She was always worrying that she was a little too curvy, but he thought she was perfect. Soft and sleek in all the right places.

"I couldn't sleep, either." He had a lot of practice suppressing his desire for her. He put it to use now, ignoring the stirring sensation in his jeans and concentrating on the fleeting expressions crossing Tara's face.

She had never been one to wear her feelings on her sleeve, and over the years she'd gotten pretty good at hiding her thoughts, even from him. He wasn't sure now if he could read her emotions, but she couldn't hide the sadness shadowing her green eyes.

He crossed to where she stood and waited. If she wanted his comfort, she'd take it.

She caught one of his hands in hers, a fleeting brush of her fingers across his. Then she dropped her hand back to her side. "I wonder if the story has made the local news," she murmured, wandering toward the hallway.

He followed her into the front room, where she sat on the sofa, picked up the remote on the coffee table and turned on the TV. He settled beside her as she started flipping channels, looking for a local news station.

He hated to tell her the story might already have made the national cable news channels by now. It was sensational enough to draw the attention of news directors looking for stories to fill their twenty-four-hour formats.

He was right. She settled on one of the cable news stations, her attention arrested by a photograph of her own face filling the screen. "Fugitive Bride" was the graphic that filled the bottom of the screen in big, blocky letters.

"Oh, lovely," she muttered.

Unfortunately, the cable station didn't have any extra information about Robert Mallory's murder, though there was plenty of innuendo about the bride's untimely disappearance. The newsreader skirted the edge of libel. Barely.

As the news host moved on to a different story, Tara turned off the TV and lowered her head to her hands. "Robert's parents must be distraught."

"I'm sure they are."

"They must believe I killed him. It's what everyone believes, right?"

"No, of course not. No one who knows you believes that."

"Not that many people know me. Do they?"

He wanted to contradict her, but what she said was true. Tara had never made it easy for people to get to know her. Even Owen, who'd been her closest friend since childhood, knew there were pieces of herself she didn't share with him and probably never would.

She was good at her job as an analyst for a global security think tank based in Brody, Virginia, just across the state line. But how many of her colleagues there really knew her? They knew her qualifications, her educational background, her experience in security analysis gained working for a defense contractor for several years right out of college.

But did they know what she liked to do when she was home alone? Did they know she was a sucker for kittens, dark chocolate and flannel pajamas? Did they know that she made lists she wouldn't throw away until she'd marked off everything written there?

Did they know there was no way in hell she'd ever have killed Robert Mallory?

"Why would someone kill Robert and kidnap you?" he asked aloud.

"I don't know."

"It seems weird, doesn't it? Kidnapping you might have made sense if they were looking for ransom. I know you said Robert wasn't rich enough for kidnapping for ransom to make sense, but his parents are. So I could see the kidnappers pressuring Robert to pay up for your release, if they knew he could ask his parents for money."

"But instead, Robert was murdered. By the same people?"

"Obviously not the same people as our kidnappers, but maybe someone they were working with?"

"But why?" Tara asked. "If kidnapping me was to collect a ransom, why on earth did they kill Robert?"

"I don't know," Owen admitted, turning to face her. He took her hands in his, squeezing them firmly. "But I promise you this—we're going to figure this out. And we're going to make sure nothing like this happens to you again."

She gave him a look somewhere between love and pity before she released his hands and rose from the sofa. She crossed to the window and gazed out at the sun-bleached lawn that stretched from the side of the house to the sheltering oaks encroaching on the farm yard.

She looked terribly, tragically alone. And not for the first time in his life, Owen wondered if she'd ever really let anyone inside her circle of one.

THE WARRANT IN HAND gave Archer Trask and his team the right to search Tara Jane Bentley's small bungalow for any firearm she might own.

As she was already a person of interest in a murder, he did not have to announce his presence before forcing entry, since doing so might give her time to flee if she was inside the home. But when he opened the front door, all optimistic notions of finding Tara Bentley hiding out at home went out the window.

The place had been trashed, top to bottom, and from the faintly sour smell in the kitchen, where the refrigerator contents lay in a spilled or broken mess across the tile floor, it hadn't happened in the past few hours.

Next to him, one of the deputies uttered a succinct profanity.

Trask got on his radio and ordered a crime scene unit to meet him at Tara Bentley's house. He didn't know if this destruction had anything to do with what had happened to Robert Mallory, but someone had tossed this place, clearly looking for something.

But what? What secrets was Ms. Bentley keeping? And did those secrets have anything to do with Mallory's death?

He stepped gingerly back through the living room at the front of the house, pausing as a framed photograph lying on the floor caught his eye. The glass was cracked, but the photo remained intact. Dark-haired Tara Bentley, grinning at the camera, leaning head-to-head with a dark-haired man with sharp blue eyes. His smile was a little less exuberant than hers, but he was clearly happy to be with her.

"Owen Stiles," Trask murmured.

"Sir?" a passing deputy asked.

"Stiles," he repeated, showing the man the photograph. "Bentley's partner in crime."

"You think the bride killed the groom and ran off with the best man?"

"Not the best man. The man of honor. He was standing up for the bride, not the groom." Trask put the photograph back on the floor where he'd found it and walked out the front door, motioning for the other deputies to follow him. They crossed back to their vehicles to wait for the crime scene unit to arrive.

Leaning against the front panel of his unmarked sedan, Trask pulled out his phone and dialed a number. A deep-voiced man with a distinctive drawl answered on the second ring. "Heller."

"Mr. Heller, it's Archer Trask. We met back in December when I was looking into the threats against Charlie Winters."

Heller's voice was wary. "I remember."

"I need to talk to you about one of your employees, Owen Stiles. I can be there later today, if you can see me?"

There was a brief pause. "Of course. Three o'clock?"

"I'll be there." He pocketed his phone and looked around the neat property, trying to picture Tara Bentley there. The place was small but well maintained. He suspected the house would have been the same if someone hadn't trashed it.

"What were they looking for, Tara?" he murmured aloud.

And where are you now?

Chapter Five

The blank notepad on the desk in front of her seemed to be taunting her. With a grimace, Tara picked up her pen and wrote a single word across the top of the pad: *Why?*

Why had those two men kidnapped her? Why had someone killed Robert? Were the two events connected?

Surely they had to be. It would be too much of a coincidence if they weren't.

She wrote those two questions beneath the header. Below that, she wrote another word: *What?*

What had the kidnappers wanted from her? What had they been planning to do with her? Ask for a ransom? Trade her for someone else, like a hostage exchange? If so, for whom?

A quiet knock on the bedroom door set her nerves rattling. "Come in," she called, turning to watch Owen enter her bedroom.

"I thought you were going to take a nap," he said.

"I tried," she lied. She hadn't tried, because the questions swirling through her head wouldn't let her rest.

The look Owen sent her way suggested he knew she was lying, but he didn't call her on it. Instead, he sat on the edge of the bed and leaned toward the desk beside it. "Making lists?"

"It's what I do."

His lips curved in a half smile, carving distinguished lines in his handsome face. He really had no idea how beautiful a man he was, but she knew. He'd been something of a late bloomer, growing into his lanky frame and thin, serious face. By the time adulthood had fulfilled the nascent promise of good looks that had only occasionally flashed into view during his awkward adolescence, his quiet nature and tendency toward shyness had already left an indelible mark on his personality.

He was brilliant at his work as a computer wizard, possibly because of his tendency to hide behind the computer screen, where he was the king of his own little world. His circle of close friends was even smaller than Tara's, and hers wasn't exactly expansive. In fact, Robert Mallory had been the first person she'd let get close to her in years. And now that he was gone, she was feeling a crushing amount of guilt at having led him on when she was beginning to admit to herself that she'd never really loved him the way she'd claimed to.

Owen picked up the notepad. "You think your kidnapping and Robert's murder are connected?"

"Do you think it's likely they're not?"

He thought for a moment before replying. "No. But damned if I can figure out what the connection might be."

Tara rubbed her gritty eyes. "That's where I am. I have no idea why anyone would have abducted me. Ransom is the usual reason, but if that was the motive, why on earth would someone kill the only person with the potential to supply the money?"

Owen's gaze narrowed. "These are the thoughts keeping you from sleep?"

She frowned. "You think that's strange?"

"I think you're avoiding what's really driving your unease."

Here we go, she thought. Owen was going to psychoanalyze her again. As usual. She leaned back in her chair and folded her arms across her chest. "I suppose you're going to tell me what I'm avoiding?"

His lips pressed into a thin line of annoyance, as she'd known they would. But his irritation didn't deter him. "Your fiancé was murdered today. You were kidnapped, rather roughly, if those bruises on your arms are any indication. But rather than deal with the fear and grief you must be feeling, you're making lists." He picked up the notepad and flipped it onto the bed beside him. "This is what you always do."

"And this is what you always do," she snapped, snatching the notepad from the bed and putting it back on the desk in front of her. "You think you know what I'm feeling and when I tell you you're wrong, you tell me I'm sublimating my emotions or something."

"Because you are."

"Says you."

"Yes," he said.

Infuriating man! She turned back to the desk and picked up her pen, determined to shut out him and his unsolicited opinions.

"I'm sorry," he said a moment later, after she'd struggled without any luck to come up with another entry for her list. "I've known you so long, I tend to think I know everything you're thinking or feeling, but obviously, I don't. So why don't you tell me about your list?"

Even though she suspected his apology was just a backdoor attempt to get back to his psychoanalysis of her emotional state, she hated when she and Owen were at odds, so she handed him the list she'd made. "Like I said, I think my kidnapping and Robert's murder have to be connected. But I don't know how."

He read over her jotted notes. "Good questions," he noted with a faint quirk of his lips. "I'll tell you what sticks out to me, if you like."

She waved her hand at him. "Please."

"What *did* they want from you? If you're right, and Robert's murder was connected to your kidnapping, then I don't think ransom could be the motive for your kidnapping."

"Agreed."

"So what would they have accomplished by kidnapping you?"

"I don't know."

"You don't have money. You're not a romantic rival someone needs to get out of the way—if Robert had some obsessive stalker, she'd have kidnapped you by herself, not hired two thugs to take you, and she probably wouldn't have killed Robert, at least not this early in the game."

"Your mind works in some really scary ways," Tara muttered.

His smile was a little wider that time. "It's part of my charm."

"Okay, so no ransom, no crazy jealous chick."

"You do have one thing that someone might want," Owen said after a brief pause. "Your work."

She frowned. "But how many people really

know what I do? Most of my friends think I'm a systems analyst, and frankly, they don't know or care what that is anyway."

"But you're a systems analyst for one of the top security and intelligence think tanks in the country—the world, in fact. And more to the point, you have a pretty astounding security clearance level for a civilian contractor. I'm your best friend in the world, and even I don't know exactly what it is you and your company are planning these days, except that it must be pretty damn big if you couldn't take a couple of weeks off for a honeymoon."

Owen was right. The project she was working on these days was huge and considered top secret in her company. Only a few people she worked with knew what her part of the job entailed, and that was on purpose, since she had been tasked with planning a supersecret security symposium that would be drawing some of the highest-ranking security and intelligence officers from friendly—and even a few not-so-friendly—nations across the globe. Not even her fiancé, Robert, knew the full scope of what she was doing these days, though he'd been insatiably curious.

She frowned, a terrible thought occurring to her. "What if Robert was killed in an attempt to find out what I was doing for my company?"

"You mean they tried to get information from him and something went wrong?"

She swallowed with difficulty. "Or they realized he didn't know anything and wasn't any use to them, so…"

"They killed him," Owen finished for her. "I suppose it's possible, if your job is really what's behind what happened today."

She rubbed her neck, where tension was building into coiling snakes of pain. "I'm so tired I can't think, but I can't seem to turn my brain off."

Owen reached out and caught her hand. "I'll give you a neck rub. That'll help, won't it?"

She met his gaze, seeing no guile there. Owen wasn't like most other men. His offers of kindness had no ulterior motives. That was one of the reasons she trusted him in a way she'd never trusted anyone else in her life, not even Robert. To Owen, a neck rub was just a neck rub.

She turned her chair until her back was in front of him. The elastic band holding her ponytail had slipped a little, so she reached up and tightened it, giving him a clear view of her neck.

A moment passed before his hands touched her neck. They were neither hot nor cold, just pleasantly warm against her flesh. He eased his way into the massage, first with light strokes that sent minute shivers rippling down her spine. But soon, his fingers pressed deeper into her muscles, eliciting a flood of pleasure-pain that sent tremors rumbling low in her belly.

A neck rub might just be a neck rub for Owen, she realized, but it had never been, and never would be, just a neck rub for her.

He wasn't anywhere near the perfect man of her wish list. He was too much the introvert, too prone to shutting out the world and burrowing into his own head when he got interested in a project. He lacked the driving ambition that might have made him the next Steve Jobs or Elon Musk. His occasional social awkwardness, which seemed to hit him at the worst possible moments, was such a contrast to the sort of social charm and ease that Robert Mallory had checked off her must-have list.

And yet he was deliciously sexy in the way that a really smart, really decent man could be. He had a wicked sense of humor and a delight in all things absurd that always seemed to be able to bring her out of even the worst mood, on those days when the weight of her world seemed insupportable. His intensely blue eyes could mesmerize her when he was talking about something he was passionate about, whether it was some intricacy of computer science she couldn't understand or his love of baseball, an obsession they shared.

And his hands. He had the best hands, long-fingered and strong, with a deft dexterity that could turn a simple neck rub into pure seduction.

"Are you being nice to me now to make up for pissing me off earlier?" She kept her tone intentionally light, struggling against his spell.

His low voice hummed against her skin. "Is it working?"

Spectacularly, she thought. "If I say yes, you might not try as hard."

"Nonsense. I always strive to do my best."

If he were anyone but Owen, she'd be seriously contemplating sex right about now, she realized. But he was Owen, and Owen was off-limits, so she eased away from his touch. "That was just what I needed. I think maybe I can get a little sleep now."

As she'd known he would, Owen stepped away from the bed. "You do that. I'll try to get some sleep myself and then if you're awake in a few hours, we'll see about something for supper."

Impulsively, she caught his hand as he turned to go and pulled him into a tight hug. His arms enfolded her, strong to her unexpectedly weak.

"It's going to be all right," he murmured against her temple. "We'll figure all this out, I promise."

She let go and covered her emotion with a soft

laugh. "We've had our share of figuring our way out of trouble, haven't we?"

He gave her ponytail a light tug. "Tara and Owen, the terrors of Mercerville."

"That was mostly me," she said wryly.

He smiled. "True."

She watched him leave the room and close the door behind him, feeling suddenly, terribly alone.

MADDOX HELLER WAS not alone in his office when Archer Trask arrived for their meeting. He took in the three people sitting in the small office space with unexpected trepidation, for he wasn't a man easily intimidated. But Heller had called in the other two chief officers of Campbell Cove Security, the enigmatic Alexander Quinn, a former CIA agent and a man who seemed to grow inexplicably more mysterious with each revelation about his past; and the elegant and beautiful Rebecca Cameron, a woman who Archer Trask knew primarily by her reputation as an accomplished diplomat and a brilliant historian. It was she who rose to greet him, extending her graceful, long-fingered hand for a shake.

"I hope you don't mind if Alexander and I join the meeting," she said with a friendly smile that brought sparkles to her dark eyes and carved handsome curves in her otherwise ageless face.

She smelled good, Trask thought, her scent delicate but intoxicating. She was probably his elder by at least five or six years, but she had a youthful grace that made him feel ancient next to her.

"Saves you the trouble of questioning us separately," Maddox drawled, flashing a quicksilver smile that Trask didn't quite buy.

More like prevents me from separating you in the effort to catch you in a discrepancy, he thought. He took the seat Maddox offered, situated in front of their chairs, subtly surrounded by them.

As if he were the one being questioned.

"How long has Owen Stiles worked for your company?" he asked before someone could interrupt to offer him coffee or some other distraction.

"Almost a year now," Quinn answered. "He was one of our earliest hires and has worked out very well."

"He's in your IT department?" Trask asked, knowing it was a leading question. He already knew Stiles worked in Cybersecurity, although even his best intel hadn't managed to uncover exactly what cybersecurity meant to a company like Campbell Cove Security. Was he an analyst? Or was he a white hat hacker of some sort?

Or perhaps both?

"He's in Cybersecurity," Quinn answered

blandly. "He analyzes security threats in both government and civilian networks and comes up with solutions to close the gaps that terrorists try to exploit."

Quinn came across as open and honest on the surface, but Trask didn't buy it. The only problem was, he wasn't sure Quinn was actually lying. He might be telling the truth, or he might be leaving out something important. Trask honestly couldn't tell.

"Do you have any idea where he is now?"

"No," Quinn answered. "We've been trying to find him, as you can imagine. He's vital to our work here, and his disappearance is troubling."

Trask narrowed his eyes, looking past Quinn to Rebecca Cameron. Her expression was as placid as the surface of a lake on a still day, reflecting her surroundings more than revealing anything beneath the surface. As for Maddox Heller, he simply shot Trask a look that was somewhere between a smile and a smirk, as if he knew exactly how frustrating this interview was turning out to be.

Clearly, they had circled the wagons around their employee, and nothing Trask asked in this particular interview would cause them to break ranks. So he changed direction.

"Do you know Tara Bentley?"

He spotted a slight flicker in Heller's expression before he pasted on that smirky smile again. "She asked Owen to be her man of honor in her wedding, so I know they're good friends."

"I believe they grew up together," Quinn offered blandly.

"Since middle school, didn't Owen say?" Cameron offered. "Sweet, to have stayed friends so many years, don't you think?"

"Have any of you met her?"

"Briefly, I think. She's come by to take him to lunch a couple of times, hasn't she?" Cameron smiled at her coworkers.

"But other than that, you know nothing about her?"

There wasn't even the briefest of pauses before Alexander Quinn answered, "No. Nothing at all."

OWEN HAD GONE to his bedroom with good intentions, but moments after he'd stretched out on the bed, the call of his computer overcame his weariness. Planting himself in front of the computer array, he considered his options.

Something had been bothering him since Maddox Heller rescued him and Tara from the road near the old Boy Scout camp. At the time, he'd been too wet, tired and hungry to ask any questions, but now that he was dry and warm, with a light lunch still filling his belly, he'd had time to realize something wasn't quite right about the situation.

For one thing, Maddox Heller had asked almost nothing about what had happened to them. He'd taken Owen's terse explanation over the phone at face value, asking no questions of any import. He'd simply accepted that Tara and Owen must be telling the truth, no matter how strange the circumstances of their abduction and despite the utter dearth of proof of their story.

Yes, he'd been their employee for a year now, but he knew that if one of the people working under him in the Cybersecurity section at Campbell Cove Security had come to him with such a strange story, he'd have asked a few more questions himself.

So why hadn't Heller?

He bypassed the normal remote desktop access to his work computer and instead decided to exploit a back door he'd created to anonymously monitor any computer activity company-wide. But to his astonishment, he found that his back door was blocked.

What the hell? Had Quinn ordered his full network access to be revoked? Why? Did he suspect Owen of something nefarious after all?

Maybe that was why Heller hadn't asked any extra questions. Maybe they were trying to contain Owen and Tara, keeping them under control in the secluded little safe house until they could finish an investigation.

He kept digging, trying other potential network access points until he managed to get back into the system through another narrow gap in security. It wouldn't take long for someone to notice the network intrusion, so he had to work fast before he was detected.

He went right to the most likely source of information—Alexander Quinn. If anything worth knowing about was going on at Campbell Cove Security, Alexander Quinn would know about it.

He was running out of time, fast, when he stumbled across a file about five levels deep in his user directory. It was hidden among Quinn's download files, though the file itself seemed to have been created in the directory rather than downloaded.

What caught Owen's eye was the file name: Jane0216.

Jane was Tara's middle name. And February 16 was her birthday.

Acutely aware of the ticking clock, Owen quickly copied the file to his personal cloud server account and backed out of the network. He was pretty sure his intrusion hadn't been detected; he'd seen no signs of anyone trying to block him out. He made a mental note to shore up the security for the network entry point as soon as he could. And he was going to do a little digging around when he got a chance to see how the cybersecurity team at Campbell Cove Security had blocked him out of his usual entry point.

But first he wanted a look at that mysterious file.

It was password protected, of course. But one of the courses Owen taught at Campbell Cove Academy was on password cracking for law enforcement. In fact, Owen had written a program for password cracking, using a set of queries that helped create a list of likely passwords based on an individual's unique set of personal connections and statistics. Of course, Quinn posed a particular problem, since both his past and present were shrouded in mystery. Owen was too smart to use the usual password prompts, but with a little creative thinking, combined with his knowledge of Quinn's past exploits, he managed to sniff out the password in a couple of hours.

"'DaresSalaamNairobi_080798,'" he read aloud with a satisfied smile. The boss had made a mistake after all, using a seminal moment in his history as a CIA agent to create his password. Quinn had once told Owen that it was August 7, 1998, not September 11, 2001, that had been the real start of Osama bin Laden's war against the United States. "He and Zawahiri killed over two hundred people in those attacks on our embassies in Tanzania and Kenya, including friends of mine. But it happened halfway around the world, so people just didn't pay attention, even though the intelligence community was practically screaming for them to wake up."

Holding his breath, Owen opened the file.

It was a background check on Tara Bentley, he saw. Detailed and intrusive, chronicling her life back to childhood. It appeared to cover all the details Owen knew about Tara and a few he didn't.

"What on earth is that?"

Tara's voice, shockingly close behind him, made him jump. He whirled around in his desk chair to look at her and found her staring at the computer screen, her eyes wide with horror.

"You have a file on me?" she asked, her pained gaze meeting his.

"Not me," he said, reaching out to take her hand, overwhelmed by the need to connect with her before she withdrew from him completely. "This isn't my file. I found it on the Campbell Cove Security network. Specifically, on my boss's computer."

"Maddox Heller?" she asked, her expression still a vivid picture of dismay. She felt violated, Owen knew, and he didn't blame her.

"No. Alexander Quinn."

"The CIA guy?" She looked confused. "Why would he be keeping a dossier on me?"

"That," Owen said, "is what we're going to find out."

Chapter Six

Weekends weren't technically days off at Campbell Cove Security. Most of the security experts who worked for the company had signed on knowing they were on call 24/7. But Alexander Quinn wasn't a heartless beast, despite his reputation. He knew several of his agents were married and many had children, and he had already seen the murky world he and his fellow agents navigated rip apart too many marriages and families. After the meeting with Archer Trask, he'd sent Heller home to his pretty wife and adorable children, and even Becky Cameron had wandered off to do whatever it was she did on her time off.

His part of the building was very quiet, though he knew there were a few classes going on in the academy section and some of the unmarried employees actually preferred to work weekends and take their days off during the week. Now and then he heard the faint tap of footsteps down a distant hall or the muffled shout coming from the academy wing, but he seemed to have the executive office area to himself.

Which was why the sound of a ding on the computer behind him sent a frisson of alarm racing through his nervous system.

He turned to look at the computer and found a query box blinking back at him.

"Why do you have a file on Tara Bentley?"

His eyes narrowing, he tapped an answer on his keyboard.

"Because she's important to you."

There was a long pause before another message popped onto the screen.

"Do you know why she was kidnapped?"

How to answer that question? In truth, while Quinn had some ideas what might be behind the woman's abduction, he didn't know anything for sure. Her work at the Security Strategies Foundation was, in part, classified, requiring a certain level of security clearance.

Technically, based on his own company's contract with the US government, Quinn's clearance was sufficient to access that level of information, but there were protocols of information sharing that would take time to work through. And unless the government deemed the situation to be a national security risk, Security Solutions could always refuse to share the information.

"I have ideas," he finally typed.

After another significant pause, another message appeared on screen. "You didn't supply us with phones. Why?"

Quinn didn't suppose Owen would buy the idea that he'd just forgotten about phones. So he told the truth. "I didn't want the two of you to try to contact anyone on the outside."

Owen's next message was blunt. "Because you haven't decided what to do with us?"

Exactly. But Owen had a point. Talking to him on the computer, without the benefit of hearing the tone of his voice, was less than informative.

"I'm coming to see you in person," he typed. "I will explain everything and we can talk strategies. I'll be there in an hour. Now get off my computer."

He waited for a reply, but no more dialogue boxes appeared on his computer screen. He finally turned back to his desk and picked up his cell phone.

Becky Cameron answered on the second ring. "Not a good time."

"I'm going to go see our guests. Don't suppose you'd like to join us?"

There was a protracted pause, then a sigh. "Actually, I'd love to. But I can't. I'm in the middle of something and can't get away. But I'm very curious to hear your thoughts about the situation. Maybe we could meet tomorrow evening? I was thinking about driving into Whitesburg to try that new Greek restaurant that just opened."

Quinn raised an eyebrow. Becky was an old friend, one of his closest, in fact, but she was almost militantly protective of her private life. He supposed she might see the dinner invitation as just a way to combine work with her need for food, but driving all the way to Whitesburg seemed a little more personal than that.

"I can meet you there," he said, more curious than he liked to admit. "Seven?"

"Perfect. I'll see you there and you can catch me up."

She had to know they couldn't talk about Owen Stiles and Tara Bentley in public that way. So what was she up to?

Despite his reputation for embracing all things enigmatic, Quinn really didn't like a mystery, especially when it involved one of his closest colleagues.

"DO YOU TRUST HIM?" Tara managed not to nibble her thumbnail as she waited for Owen's reply. She'd spent most of her teen years trying to break her nail-biting habit and she'd be danged if she started doing it again now. She might be hiding from both kidnappers and the law, but that was no excuse for bad grooming.

"I don't know."

Owen was cleaning the kitchen counters, even though they were virtually spotless. It was his version of nail biting, she supposed, though he generally fine-tuned his computer rather than cleaned the house when he was puzzling over a troubling problem. She supposed the new computer system was too state-of-the-art to provide him quite enough distraction for their current dilemma.

"That's not reassuring," she said.

He stopped wiping the counter long enough to offer her a halfhearted grin. "I know."

"He used to be with the CIA. Which could be a good thing or a very bad thing."

"The problem with Quinn, in my admittedly limited experience, is that he's a big-picture guy. He's going to look out for the country first, his company next and then individuals fall in line behind those two things. Which is why I began to suspect Quinn may think what happened to us is connected to something bigger."

Such as the symposium she was supposed to be planning. The event so important that she and Robert had planned to postpone their honeymoon until late summer so she could get things done.

Tara perched on the bar stool in front of the counter Owen had resumed cleaning, taking care not to leave fingerprints on the nice, shiny surface. "There's something I've been doing at work that has been my entire focus for months now. Nobody else knows all the details except for me and the company's operating officers. Now I'm no longer there to do the job. What does that do to the equation?"

"You tell me." Owen stopped wiping and draped the towel over the edge of the sink. "If something happens to you, who takes over your job?"

"It would have to be one of the three partners. They were very careful to keep all the information about my project secret, with good reason."

Curiosity gleamed in his bright blue eyes, but he didn't ask her anything about her project. "So that's why you postponed the honeymoon."

"Yes."

"Could someone outside the company know what you were planning?" he asked.

"Yes, of course. It involves other people outside the company, and any of them could have experienced an intelligence leak. But that's one reason why the details of the project were so closely guarded. Even if someone found out what was going on, they wouldn't have the vital details to work with because those details won't be settled until about a week before it comes together."

"So it's an event."

"Owen, I can't tell you anything else. I'm sorry."

He smiled. "Understood. But if it's an event, then perhaps someone wants to sabotage it in some way. Would that be a possibility?"

She didn't reply, but Owen's expression suggested he'd read the answer in her face.

"Maybe that was the point of the abduction," he suggested. "To get the information out of you under duress. Or am I being too dramatic here?"

"It's possible," she admitted. "Without going into details, it's very possible that someone would like to get his hands on the information I have. I'm a more vulnerable target than any of the directors of the company would be, and nobody else has the information."

At the time the directors had approached her to run the project, she was over-the-moon delighted about the responsibility, knowing it meant the company valued her organizational and analytical skills as well as her reliability and discretion. While she'd consulted with the directors regularly, they'd allowed her to take the reins as far as planning the logistics of the symposium was concerned. She'd been the point person with all the countries and dignitaries invited, the face of their very prestigious think tank.

But now she was beginning to realize the steep price that such a high-profile position of authority could exact. The job had quite possibly made her a target.

She might still be a target, she realized. Her disappearance and the mystery surrounding Robert's murder would likely cause her bosses to shore up their already tight security. The kidnappers would have a difficult time getting through their defenses.

But she was still largely defenseless. If Owen hadn't come to her aid, she probably wouldn't have been able to escape the kidnappers. But even that situation had been nothing more than pure luck. The kidnappers had underestimated their resourcefulness, and they hadn't prepared for Owen's surprise arrival. They'd also been sloppy, binding her hands in front of her instead of behind her. She doubted they'd be that careless a second time.

While she'd been pondering her vulnerability, Owen had put up the cleaning supplies and washed his hands in the sink. He turned to her now, drying his hands on a paper towel, his eyes narrowed. It was his "I wonder what you're thinking" expression, and she realized that she was far more tempted right now to tell him everything about her secret project than she'd ever been with Robert.

She supposed that was the difference between a whirlwind romance and twenty years of enduring and unbreakable friendship. That fact only made her more certain than ever that she'd made the right choice when she began feeling attracted to Owen. Boyfriends were unpredictable and, in her experience, undependable.

Owen was her rock. It was a mistake to sleep with your rock.

Wasn't it?

A sharp rap on the door rattled her nerves. Owen tossed the paper towel in the waste bin and headed for the front door. Tara trailed behind him, her heart pounding with anxiety.

Owen checked the security lens. "It's Quinn. You ready?"

Tara took a couple of deep, bracing breaths and nodded. "Ready."

Owen opened the door to a broad-shouldered man with sandy hair and intelligent eyes the color of dried moss. He wore a neatly groomed beard a couple of shades darker than his hair and liberally sprinkled with silver. He looked to be in his midforties, but in his eyes Tara saw an old soul, a man whose life had been one struggle after another. The weight of the world was reflected not in lines on his face but in the shadowy depths of those hazel-green eyes.

He was dangerous, Tara realized with a flutter of alarm. But he also seemed like someone who'd be invaluable in a fight, as long as you were on the same side.

He was not an enemy she wanted to make.

"You must be Tara Bentley." Quinn shook hands with a firm, brisk grip. "I've heard a good deal about you."

"You've mean you've snooped around my life and uncovered a great deal about me," Tara corrected, her voice edged with tart disapproval.

"Fair enough." Quinn nodded toward the sofa. "Shall we sit and talk?"

TARA SAT IN the armchair, leaving Quinn and Owen to share the sofa. It put her at a slightly elevated angle, which made her feel more in control of the situation. "Do you know why we were kidnapped?"

Quinn's lips quirked slightly. It wasn't quite a smile, but there was a hint of humor in his eyes. "I believe it might have something to do with your work at Security Solutions."

"And why was Robert killed?"

"I don't know." His voice softened. "My condolences on your loss."

"Thank you."

"What do you know about my job?" Tara asked.

"I contacted your company directors and explained my concerns about my cybersecurity director disappearing along with their top analyst. We had an illuminating discussion about the work you've been doing."

"Why would they tell you anything illuminating?" Tara asked, wary of being tricked into revealing more than she should.

"Because I have a security clearance as high as theirs. I'm a security contractor for the government. I know things that few federal employees know about the government's security apparatus."

"Do I need to go take a walk so you can speak freely?" Owen asked, starting to rise.

"No," Quinn said. "Your own security clearance is high enough for you to hear what Ms. Bentley and I have to say."

"You first," Tara said as Owen sat again.

The quirk returned to Quinn's lips, a little broader this time. Definitely his version of a smile, Tara thought. He inclined his head slightly toward Tara before he spoke. "Your bosses didn't give me the details of the project, of course, for the sake of situational security. But I know that you're planning a global symposium on new terror tactics and strategies for preventing them from succeeding. You've invited over seventy nations to participate. I don't know where or even when the meeting will take place, but I know it's going to happen on US soil, and someone very much wants to know the details."

"Which is why they kidnapped Tara," Owen murmured.

"Yes." Quinn looked at Tara, his expression hard to read. "You are the most wanted woman in a lot of terror-sponsoring countries. Any number of groups, foreign and domestic, would love to get their hands on the information you know. Your bosses at Security Solutions don't know why or how you disappeared, so obviously they're deeply worried. It's not just the local authorities who are looking for you."

"I have to turn myself in, then," Tara said.

Quinn cleared his throat before he spoke. "That does seem to be the best course of action."

"I didn't kill Robert."

"I know that. And there's no evidence to connect you to his murder. I think at this point, you're primarily wanted for questioning, just to clear up why you disappeared and where you've been."

"We can't provide any evidence of what happened to us," Owen warned. "All we have is our word."

"And you're not a disinterested witness," Quinn agreed. "But neither of you has any reason to kill Robert. Since no marriage had taken place, there's no profit motive for Ms. Bentley. There's not a whiff of conflict between the two of you, according to interviews with Robert's family and your friends. It's not like you and Owen are secret lovers who killed your fiancé so you could run away together."

Tara glanced at Owen. "No."

There was a flicker of something in Quinn's eyes as he looked from her to Owen. "Is there anything I need to know about the events of yesterday that either of you haven't already told me?"

"There is one thing," Tara said, "although nobody knows about it but Owen and me. I was planning to call off the wedding right before I was abducted."

"I see."

"Owen didn't know beforehand," she added. "I didn't tell him until after we escaped."

"I suspected," Owen said. "She called me and—"

"The less I know about that, the better," Quinn interrupted. "If you don't have a lawyer, Campbell Cove Security can provide one."

"Thank you. That would be helpful," Tara said. "How will this work?"

"I think, because of the threats against your life, we shouldn't schedule the time to turn yourself in. You, Owen and the lawyer will show up unannounced at the Bagley County Sheriff's Department and ask for Deputy Archer Trask, the investigator in charge of the Robert Mallory homicide investigation. The element of surprise will be your best safeguard against a repeat of yesterday's abduction attempt."

Tara glanced at Owen. He met her gaze with an almost imperceptible nod. She looked at Quinn again. "Okay. That sounds good."

"Tomorrow morning would be best. Get a good night's sleep, take time to shower, shave and dress in your Sunday best. You're the victims, not the perpetrators. You need to be confident and at ease. I'll return in the morning with your lawyer, we'll go over the case and then we'll drive you to town."

"Sounds like a plan," Owen said with a faint smile.

Quinn flashed that half quirk of a smile toward Owen. "You did well, under difficult circumstances. We will get you both through the rest of this."

"Thank you."

She and Owen walked with Quinn to the door. He turned in the open doorway, his features dark and indistinct against the bright afternoon sun. "We'll do everything in our power to protect you, Ms. Bentley. Know that."

"Thank you. I appreciate it." She watched,

her heart thudding heavily in her chest, as if his words had been a warning instead of a promise.

She was a target. She'd known the possibility existed, but until Quinn had said the words aloud, the notion had been just that. A notion, something possible but not certain.

Now the cloud of threat hanging over her head felt heavy with foreboding, as if she were trapped without any hope of escape.

The touch of Owen's hands on her shoulders made her jump. She turned to look at him and felt the full intensity of his blue-eyed gaze.

"We will get through this. Tomorrow, we'll turn ourselves in and the police will protect you."

"What if they can't? It's a small county in a small state. They're not prepared or trained to provide protection from determined terrorists."

"Then Quinn will put agents in place to watch your back." The visit from his boss had apparently shored up Owen's defenses. He sounded strong and confident, and the firmness of his grip on her shoulders seemed to transfer that sense of strength into her, so that by the time he let her go and nodded for her to precede him into the hallway, she felt steadier herself.

Maybe everything really would be okay.

OWEN STOOD OUTSIDE the groom's room, trying to gather his courage to go inside. On the other side of the door stood the man who was about to take Tara away from him, and he was supposed to be wishing him good luck.

How could he do it? How could he shake Robert's hand and tell him to take care of the woman Owen loved more than anyone else in the world? How was he supposed to be okay with any of this?

Do it because Tara needs you to. Do it because it's the only way you'll be able to stay in her life.

His heart pounded wildly. His palms were damp with sweat. Though he'd met Robert dozens of times since he first started dating Tara, the man had remained little more than an acquaintance. There had always been a wary distance between them, as if Robert understood that Owen would never really be all right with his presence in Tara's life. And Robert would never truly be comfortable with how important Owen was to Tara, either.

But if they both wanted to stay in her life, they were going to have to create some sort of truce, however wary and fragile it might be.

He took a deep breath and reached for the door.

But a scraping noise from within the room stopped him midstep. The world around him seemed to disintegrate, and he was suddenly lying on his back, darkness pressing in one him, heavy and cold. It took a moment to realize he was in an unfamiliar bed in an unfamiliar place.

The safe house. He'd been dreaming. Groping for the small digital clock on the bedside table, he squinted to see the time. Only a little after eight, he saw with surprise.

As he rubbed his eyes, he heard another faint scrape of metal on metal. It seemed to be coming from the front of the house.

Tara? Maybe she hadn't been able to sleep.

But when he rose from the bed, he grabbed the unloaded Smith & Wesson .380 from the locked box he'd stashed in the bedside table drawer. He'd put the ammo in the dresser across the room, the way he'd been trained—don't keep the ammo with the gun. The rule had always seemed reasonable to him, as it would make it hard for an intruder to load the gun and use it against him. But now that he was trying to go out and face a potential threat, the extra step seemed to slow him down.

He had to protect Tara, even if it meant carrying a gun and facing the unknown.

Heart pounding wildly, he opened the bedroom door.

Chapter Seven

A furtive sound roused Tara from slumber. She sat upright in bed, her pulse roaring in her ears. Straining to hear past the whoosh of blood through her veins, she tried to remember what, exactly, she'd heard. Was it a scrape? A tap? It hadn't been as loud as a knock.

It's an old house, she told herself. Old houses made noise. A lot.

Then she heard the noise again. It was a scrape, like metal against metal. It came not from her room but from somewhere down the hall.

Someone trying to enter the front door?

Suddenly, Owen seemed an impossible distance away, even though his bedroom was just across the hall. She didn't think the sound was coming from there, but with her door closed, it was impossible to know for certain.

Owen had the gun. She hoped to goodness he really did know how to use it.

She eased her bedroom door open, holding her breath at the soft creak of the hinges. In the distance, thunder rumbled, and for a moment Tara wondered if it had been the gathering storm that had wakened her so suddenly. But it had barely been audible at all, certainly not loud enough to stir her from a dead sleep. And the noise she'd heard earlier definitely hadn't been thunder.

She slipped out into the hallway, the wood floors smooth and cool beneath her feet. The temperature had fallen along with the night, and she shivered as she crept across to Owen's room.

As she reached for the door handle, it twisted in her hand, startling her. She jerked back, stumbling over her own feet.

In the murky gloom, she felt as if she were tumbling backward into an abyss, the world turned upside down.

Then arms wrapped around her, stilling her fall. Owen's arms, his familiar scent unmistakable. He pulled her tightly to his bare chest, his own heart galloping beneath her ear as he held her close.

The moment seemed to stretch into infinity, as all her senses converged into an exquisite flood of desire. His skin was hot silk beneath her hands as she clutched his arms. He smelled like soap and Owen, a clean, masculine essence that had always made her feel safe and happy, even when the world around her was going crazy. The bristle of his crisp chest hair rasped against her breasts beneath the thin fabric of her tank top, bringing her nipples to hard, sensitive peaks.

She forced herself to shut down all those sensations, the way she'd been doing since she turned fifteen and began to realize that the gangly boy next door was becoming an attractive young man.

"Did you hear the noise?" Owen whispered, his voice barely breath against her hair.

She nodded.

He eased her away from him, and in the flash of lightning that strobed through the window at the end of the hall, she saw the gleam of gunmetal in his hand as he slipped down the hall toward the front of the house.

She stayed close behind him, unwilling to allow him to confront whatever danger lurked ahead alone. She might not have been trained for danger the way he had been, but she was fit, she was resourceful and if she'd let herself admit it, she was also angry as all get-out.

She might not have loved Robert the way a

wife should, but he was a good man. A sweet man. He hadn't deserved to die, and the thought that he'd taken a bullet because someone was after her made her want to break things. Starting with the killer's head.

Owen paused in the doorway to the living room, and Tara had to stumble to a sharp halt to keep from barreling into him. Reaching behind him, he caught her hand briefly, gave it a squeeze, then entered the larger room.

The scraping noise came again, louder this time. It was coming from outside the house.

"Stay here," Owen whispered urgently. "I need to know you're not in the line of fire."

Her instincts told her to ignore his command, but she made herself stay still, pressing her back against the living room wall as he edged closer to the front door and took a quick look through the peephole in the door.

He backed away, glancing back at her. He shook his head.

Outside, the wind had picked up again, moaning in the eaves. The first patter of rain on the metal roof overhead was loud enough to set Tara's nerves jangling. Owen crossed quietly to where she stood, rubbing her upper arms gently. "I'm pretty sure it's the wind rattling something outside. Maybe a loose gutter or a window screen. I don't see anyone lurking around."

"They wouldn't be out in the open, would they?"

"Probably not." He glanced back toward the door.

She followed his gaze. It was an ordinary wooden door, but somehow, in the dark, with her heart racing and her skin tingling, it seemed more like an ominous portal to a dangerous realm. "Someone could be trying to lure us outside."

"Or we could be letting our imaginations run away with us, the same way we used to do sneaking around Old Man Ridley's cabin twenty years ago," he countered. "I really do think it's just the wind."

She let out a huff of nervous laughter. "You're probably right."

"The only way to figure that out is to go outside and try to find the source of the sound. Do you want me to do that?"

Part of her wanted to say yes, just so she'd know one way or the other. But it was cold and rainy, and even if there were a threat outside, which she was starting to doubt, they were safer inside than outside.

"No," she said. "I think you're right. It's just the wind rattling something outside. I'm sorry for being such a scaredy-cat."

"You want to try going back to bed and ignoring all the creaks and scrapes outside?"

"Could we maybe light a fire here in the living room and camp out on the sofa instead?"

His lips curved. "We could do that. Let me grab a shirt and a blanket."

"I'll pop some popcorn," she said, starting to finally feel a little more relaxed.

Owen had a way of making everything a little easier to bear.

OWEN WOKE IN STAGES, first vaguely aware of light on the other side of his closed eyelids, then of a warm body tucked firmly against his side. Tara, he thought, his eyes still closed. He could smell the scent of shampoo in her hair and the elusive essence of the woman herself. The soft warmth of her body against his felt perfect and necessary, as if it were an extension of himself he couldn't bear to live without.

He opened his eyes to morning sunlight angling through the east-facing front windows of the farmhouse. He'd left his watch in the bedroom, but that much light had to mean the day was well under way.

Giving Tara a gentle nudge, he said, "Wake up, sleepyhead."

She grumbled and burrowed deeper into the cocoon formed by his side and the sofa.

"It's probably after eight. Quinn and the lawyer will be here soon."

She gave a muffled groan against his side and added a soft curse for emphasis. "I was having the best dream," she complained, lifting her head and looking at him through strands of her hair.

Even makeup-free, with her normally tidy brown hair mussed and tangled, and her morning breath not quite as sweet as the rest of her, she was still the most desirable woman he'd ever known. His morning erection became almost painfully hard.

She shook her hair away from her face and stared at him, too closely curled against his body to have missed his physical response to her nearness. He waited for her to make a joke and roll off the sofa to make her escape to the bedroom, but she didn't move, her eyes darkening as exquisite tension lengthened between them.

"I don't know what I'd do if I didn't have you," she whispered.

This was the point where he would crack a joke and make his escape, but he was pinned between her and the sofa. And even if he weren't, he didn't think he'd have been capable of moving away from her luscious heat, especially when she reached out with one slim hand and touched his jaw.

He couldn't find his voice. Didn't want to risk

saying anything that would ruin this moment. It felt as if he were standing on the edge of a cliff, ready to jump into a beautiful void. What lay below might be a crystalline sea, cool and cleansing, with a whole universe of wonders and pleasures lying just beneath the surface. Or he might find himself dashed on sharp rocks to lie bleeding and dying for his gamble.

What was it going to be?

From somewhere in the back of the house, two alarm clocks went off with a loud, discordant blare.

Tara and Owen both laughed, snapping the tension of the moment. "We'd better get moving," she suggested, rolling off the sofa and straightening her tank top and shorts.

He pushed to his feet, shifting his own shorts to hide the worst of his erection. "How about scrambled eggs for breakfast?"

"We need something a little more decadent," she said, pausing in the doorway of her bedroom. "I'll make French toast."

Not exactly the sort of decadence he'd been thinking about when he woke up in her arms, but he could make do.

By the time he got out of the shower, he could smell eggs cooking from down the hallway. He laid out one of the suits he'd found in the closet, hoping it would fit, but went to the kitchen in fresh boxer shorts under a shin-length black silk robe.

"Are you worried about today?" she asked as she flipped a couple of the egg-crusted pieces of bread onto a plate and handed it to him.

"A little." He set the plate on the small breakfast nook table and retrieved the bottle of syrup from the refrigerator. "I know we didn't do anything wrong, but we don't have any real proof of our story."

She brought her own plate of French toast to the table and sat across from him. "I have half a wedding dress."

"Which could have been torn in any number of ways." He handed her the syrup bottle. "But you really didn't have any motive to kill Robert."

"What if they think you did?"

He paused with his fork halfway to his mouth. Syrup dribbled on the table and he put down the fork and grabbed a napkin. "Because you and I are so close?"

"Best friends forever." She managed a weak smile. "You know people have always mistaken us as a couple. Ever since high school."

Their closeness had broken up more than one of his romantic relationships over the years. Not without reason. "But we've only ever been friends."

"Because we choose to be only friends. But

we both know there's an attraction between us that we could build on if we ever chose it. Robert knew it. He just realized that I wasn't ever going to risk my friendship with you that way, so he didn't feel threatened." A cloud drifted over her expression. "He was remarkably understanding."

Owen wasn't sure that understanding would have lasted. Or that he could have allowed the status quo between him and Tara to continue once she was married.

Which, he supposed, *makes me a viable suspect in Robert's murder.*

THE LAWYER ALEXANDER QUINN provided was younger than Tara had expected. Anthony Giattina was tall, broad shouldered and sandy haired. He spoke with a mild southern accent and there was a sparkle in his brown eyes as he shook hands with her and Owen after Alexander Quinn's introduction.

"Call me Tony," he said. "I think we can get this handled with a minimum of fuss."

"Has Mr. Quinn told you what happened?"

"I told him I wanted to talk to each of you first. So I know the basics from news reports— your fiancé was murdered and you disappeared." His eyes softened. "My condolences."

"Thank you."

"We need to get on the road," Quinn interrupted. "You'll ride with Tony so you can talk in private. I'll follow." He nodded toward the two vehicles in the driveway and started walking toward them. He got behind the wheel of a large black SUV while Tony Giattina led them to a sleek silver Mercedes sedan parked behind Quinn's vehicle.

Owen waved Tara to the front seat and settled in the back behind her.

"So, from the beginning," Tony said after they were on the road. "Did either of you witness anything connected to Robert Mallory's murder?"

"No," Tara answered. "I didn't."

"I didn't, either," Owen said.

Tony's gaze flicked toward the backseat. "You sound uncertain."

"I saw him briefly when I arrived at the church," Owen said in a careful tone that made Tara turn to look at him, as well. "I was planning to talk to him before the wedding. Wish him well, that sort of thing. But I got the call from Tara before I could enter the groom's room."

"The call from Tara?" Tony asked.

"I was having cold feet," Tara confessed. "I called Owen because I wasn't sure I was doing the right thing, and he's always been my best sounding board."

"And what did the two of you decide?"

"I had no part in it," Owen said. "She told me

nothing was wrong and hung up before I could ask her more questions. That's why I was on the way to the bride's room when I spotted what I now know was Tara going out to the parking lot."

"Runaway bride?" Tony arched one sandy eyebrow in Tara's direction.

"No. A man knocked on the bride's room door, and when I answered he told me there was a delivery outside for me."

"And you went with him?"

"I thought it might be a misdirected wedding gift."

"And was there a delivery?"

"No. As soon as I got outside, someone put an ether-soaked pillowcase over my head and threw me into a panel van."

There was a long moment of silence as Tony digested what she'd told him. He finally cleared his throat and spoke. "Go on."

She was beginning to lose him, she realized. Of course she was. She and Owen had both realized early on that their story sounded like pure fantasy.

"I think it was at that point that I happened upon the scene," Owen said before she could speak. "I saw two men pushing Tara into the van. I ran to try to stop them, but one of them punched me and I slammed headfirst into the van. I lost consciousness at that point and didn't come to until sometime later, inside the van. My hands were bound behind my back with duct tape."

"I see," Tony said in a tone that suggested he didn't see at all. "For how long were you in the van?"

"I'm not sure. It might have been an hour or more. We ended up about twenty minutes away from the church, though, so I think maybe the men driving the van took a twisty route, maybe to be sure nobody had seen them and taken chase."

"You think."

"I can't be sure. We weren't able to hear them plotting their next move or anything like that." Owen's voice took on a sharp edge. "Look, I can tell you're skeptical of what we're saying. Maybe you're not the lawyer we need."

"You're going to have to sell your story to people a lot more skeptical than I. And I never said I don't believe you."

Tara glanced at Owen. He met her gaze with a furrowed brow.

"How did you manage to get free?"

"I got the pillowcase off Tara's head. They'd left it on when they threw her in the van, so I guess they were hoping it would keep her sedated for the trip." Owen's voice darkened. "The idiots could have killed her."

"When I woke, I was a little disoriented from the ether. My hands were tied in front of me," she said.

"Their mistake," Owen murmured, his voice warm. "They didn't anticipate both of us waking up and working together, I think."

"Do you have any idea who took you or why?"

"We're not sure," Tara said quickly. "We're both wondering if it was connected to Robert's murder."

Tony slanted a look toward her. "You're taking his death well."

She looked down at her hands, which were twisting around each other in her lap. She stilled their movement. "I don't think it's real to me yet. I didn't see his body. Maybe if I did..."

"The police will be wondering why you're so composed."

She looked up sharply at the lawyer. "Do you want me to pretend to be hysterical?"

"No, of course not."

"I cared about Robert. I loved him. I can't even wrap my brain around the idea that he's gone."

"You said you were having cold feet."

She glanced at Owen. He was looking down at his own hands, his expression pensive.

"I was going to call off the wedding."

"Why?"

"Because I realized that I wasn't in love with him. Not the way I should have been if I were going to marry him."

"Did he know that?"

"No. The kidnapper grabbed me first."

"I see." Tony tapped his thumbs on the steering wheel. "Why do you suppose the kidnappers took Owen into the van rather than killing him and leaving him in the parking lot?"

"I have no idea," she answered.

"I suppose a body in the parking lot would have raised an alert sooner than the kidnappers planned," Owen added.

"A body in the groom's room raised the alert quickly enough."

"Hidden behind a door, not out in the open in a church parking lot," Owen pointed out.

"I wonder if they were planning to use you as leverage against me," Tara murmured.

Owen looked at her, his gaze intense.

"Leverage to do what?" Tony asked, sounding curious.

"Whatever they kidnapped me for. Anyone who knows anything about me knows about my friendship with Owen. We've been nearly inseparable since sixth grade. We went to the same schools, including college. On purpose. Maybe they realized they could use him against me, to force me to do whatever it was they wanted from me."

"And you really have no idea what that could be?" Tony sounded unconvinced.

"It's all a mystery to me," Tara answered.

Tony fell silent after that, though Tara suspected the mind behind those brown eyes was hard at work, figuring out all the legal angles of their dilemma.

She hoped it would be enough.

Within a couple of minutes, they were entering Mercerville, the Bagley County seat. The sheriff's department was located in the east wing of the city hall building, with its own entrance and parking area. Tony pulled the Mercedes into an empty visitor parking spot and cut the engine.

"I'm going to call the lead investigator on the case now. I want him to meet us at the door. I don't want to just walk in unannounced."

"Quinn said we shouldn't give them any notice we were coming."

"You want to be sure you meet with the lead investigator. That requires a courtesy call ahead of time to be sure he's here. We don't want to be handed off to someone down the food chain." He made the call. From what Tara could glean from his end of the call, the lead investigator was in and would meet them at the door.

Tony ended the call and turned to face them both. "Don't offer any information they haven't asked for. Nothing. Understood? If a question confuses you, let me know and we'll stop the interviews to confer. If I think the questioning is treading on dangerous territory for you, I'll step in. Agreed?"

"Yes," Owen said.

"Agreed." Tara looked at Owen. He met her gaze with a half smile that didn't erase the anxious expression in his eyes. She felt a flutter of guilt for her part in putting Owen in this position. If she hadn't been so stupid as to leave the safety of the church with a stranger—

Movement outside the car caught her eye. Turning her head, she spotted a man in the tan uniform of a Bagley County sheriff's deputy. He was tall and broad shouldered, with a slight paunch and a slightly hitching gait that seemed familiar. As he reached the sheriff's department entrance, he turned his head toward the parking lot.

She sucked in a sharp breath.

Owen put his hand on her shoulder. "What is it?"

"That deputy." She nodded toward the front of the building, where the deputy had just pulled open the door.

"What about him?" Tony asked.

"That's the man who lured me out to the van."

Chapter Eight

Owen had seen only a flash of square jaw and a long, straight nose as the deputy disappeared through the glass door of the sheriff's department, but it was enough to send adrenaline racing through his system. The skin at the back of his neck prickled and his muscles bunched in preparation. Fight or flight, he thought, remembering the lessons of his threat response classes at Campbell Cove Academy.

Flight, his instinct commanded. He was outgunned and on the defensive here.

"Let's get out of here," he growled to Tony.

"What? Are you insane?" Tony turned to stare at him. "You came here to turn yourself in to the authorities. If you leave now, you're just going to make things worse."

"Owen's right." Tara's voice was deep and intense. "If that man is a cop, they will never believe us over him. You know how it works."

"You can't know that—"

Owen snapped open his seat belt and tried to unlock the back door of the car, but the child-safety locks were engaged. "Unlock the door," he demanded.

Tony shook his head. "I'm telling you as your lawyer, this is insane."

"You're fired." Tara reached across the console and grabbed the key fob dangling from the ignition. Before Tony Giattina could stop her, she pressed one of the buttons and the lock beside Owen made an audible click. He opened the door and exited the car.

Cool spring air filled his lungs, dispelling the faint feeling of claustrophobia he'd experienced while trapped inside the backseat. Tara was already out the passenger door, turning to him with wide eyes.

"What now?"

Owen looked back at the black SUV that had followed them to the sheriff's department. Quinn was already stepping out of the vehicle, his gaze sharp, as if he could sense the rise in tension. If anyone knew the danger they were in, it was Quinn, Owen realized. His wily boss understood that, sometimes, playing by the rules could get you killed.

Grabbing Tara's hand, he started resolutely toward the SUV.

Quinn's eyes narrowed at their approach. When Owen was close enough, Quinn muttered, "Hit me."

Owen's steps faltered. "What?"

"Hit me," Quinn said, taking a step forward. "I can't help you openly, but you can't go in there."

"How do you know..."

Quinn tapped the earpiece barely visible in his ear. "Hit me, damn it."

Without another second's hesitation, Owen let go of Tara's hand and punched Quinn as hard as he dared. His boss sprawled backward into the front panel of the SUV, his keys falling to the ground beside him.

As Owen bent to pick them up, Quinn murmured, "Not the safe house. It's compromised now. There's a stash of cash in the glove box. Use it and try to get in touch when you can." Shaking his head in a show of grogginess, he dragged himself clear of the SUV's wheels.

Tony Giattina was out of the Mercedes, his phone to his ear. Probably calling in the escape attempt, Owen realized, which meant they had only seconds before half the sheriff's department would be pouring through the doors into the parking lot.

"Let's go," he growled as he opened the front door of the SUV. Tara climbed into the passenger seat and turned to look at him, her expression terrified.

"Maybe I was wrong," she said, sounding far less confident than she had seemed a few moments earlier.

"You weren't," he assured her, putting the SUV in Reverse. He cut off a car approaching from the left, earning an angry horn blow, and headed east on Old Cumberland Road. He could take a few twisty back roads over Murlow Mountain and reach the Virginia border in less than an hour.

But what then?

"They'll have an APB out on this car in no time," Tara muttered, fastening her seat belt. "They'll scan our license plate and we'll be done for."

She was right. He had to switch the plates with another vehicle. Preferably another black SUV, but any vehicle would do, at least for a while.

Meanwhile, he stuck to the twisty mountain roads that wound their way slowly but steadily eastward toward the state line. He'd traveled with his brother in Virginia a couple of years earlier and had learned, to his surprise, that travelers could overnight in their vehicles at rest stops. That would give them accommodations for tonight, at least, until they could figure out what to do next.

But first, he needed to find a big shopping center where they could pick up supplies.

"Is anyone following us?" Tara twisted around in her seat, nibbling her thumbnail as she peered at the road behind them.

"I don't see anyone, but I'm not exactly an expert at tailing. Or being tailed."

Tara looked at him. "Do you have a plan?"

"Yes, but I'm not sure you're going to be thrilled about it."

"Better spill, then."

"Did you know that it's legal to overnight at public rest areas in Virginia?"

"Please tell me that's a non sequitur."

"I'm going to stick to back roads for another hour or so. Then I'm going to drive down to Abingdon. I think there's probably some sort of shopping center there where we can pick up some supplies—food, blankets, water."

"Those had better be thick blankets," Tara muttered.

"I'm not sure what to do about the license plates, though."

"You'd think, with your boss being a former superspy, he'd have extra license plates stashed in the trunk or something."

Owen slanted a quick look at her. "Do you think?"

"I don't know. He's your boss."

Even after a year, Owen knew very little about two of his three bosses. Maddox Heller was an open book, garrulous and friendly. His pretty wife and his two cute kids visited often, and the previous summer, Heller had invited everyone in the company out to their house on Mercer Lake for a Labor Day cookout.

But Rebecca Cameron was a very private person, despite her friendly, good-natured disposition. And Alexander Quinn was a positive enigma.

However, if there was one thing Owen knew about his inscrutable boss, it was that the man always seemed prepared for any eventuality. Including the possibility of having to go on the run at a moment's notice.

There were very few turnoffs on the curvy mountain road they were traveling, but within a few minutes, Owen spotted a dirt road on the right and slowed to turn, hoping he wasn't driving them into a dead-end trap.

"What are you doing?" Tara asked.

"I'm going to find out if Alexander Quinn is as wily as he seems."

Almost as soon as they took the turn, the dirt road hooked sharply to the right. Owen eased into the turn and the SUV was immediately swallowed by the woods, which hid not only the road from their view but, more important, hid them from the view of the road.

He pulled to a stop and cut the engine. "If you wanted to stash something secret in this SUV, where would you start?"

"The glove compartment is too obvious," Tara said.

"Quinn did tell me there was stash of cash in there."

Tara opened the glove box. Inside was a wallet, weather-beaten and fat. She pulled it out and opened the wallet. "Lots of receipts," she said as she riffled through the papers inside. "And a ten-dollar bill. I don't know your boss well, but if this is what he thinks qualifies as a stash of cash…"

Owen unbuckled his seat belt and leaned over to look. The distracting scent of Tara's skin almost made him forget what he was looking for, but he managed to gather his wits enough to search the glove compartment. Besides the wallet, there was only the car registration, a card providing proof of insurance, and a thick vehicle manual.

But Quinn had clearly told him there was a stash of cash in the glove compartment. Was this some sort of trap? A test?

He sat back a moment, thinking hard. Assuming Quinn had been playing things straight, why would he have said there was cash in the glove box if there wasn't?

Narrowing his eyes, he leaned over and looked into the glove compartment again. There could be no cash hiding in the registration paper or the insurance card. But what about the manual?

"What are you doing?" Tara asked, leaning forward until her head was right next to Owen's in front of the open compartment.

Owen turned to look at her, his breath catching at her closeness. Her green eyes seemed large and luminous as her eyebrows rose in two delicate arches.

He forced his gaze back to the glove compartment and pulled out the manual. Easing back to his own side of the SUV, he opened the manual.

There was a fifty-dollar bill slipped between the first two pages.

He flipped through the book, a smile curving his mouth. Nearly every page sandwiched money. Dozens of tens, about that many twenties, several fifties and even a handful of hundreds. Nearly five thousand dollars in cash, Owen realized after adding up the sums in his head.

"Does he usually carry that much money in his vehicle?" Tara asked when Owen told her the sum.

"I have no idea." He handed her the manual

full of money. "Leave it in there for now. I'm going to see what else I can find in this SUV."

"I'll check up here in the cab," Tara said as he opened the driver's door. "You see if there are any underfloor compartments."

Fifteen minutes later, they had uncovered a set of Tennessee license plates, another fifty dollars in change hidden in various places around the SUV, a Louisville Slugger baseball bat, a small smartphone with a prepaid phone card taped to its back, a duffel bag full of clothing and survival supplies and a dozen MREs—military-issued meals that could be prepared without cooking utensils or even a fire.

"He likes to cover all his bases," Tara said, looking at their bounty.

"I'll switch out the license plate and put the Kentucky one in the compartment where I found the Tennessee plates," Owen said. "Then I'm going to see if there are any minutes left on that phone."

"Do you think that's a good idea?"

"It's a burner phone. Quinn said to get in touch when we could. I think this is how we're supposed to do it."

Tara shook her head. "Not this soon. The police might be keeping an eye on him. Let's wait a day or two before we call him."

Owen gave her a considering look. "Okay. You're right."

"Don't sound so shocked." She shot him a quick grin. "Go change the tags and I'll see if I can find any more treasures."

Owen took a screwdriver from the small tool-box inside Quinn's survival kit and switched out the Kentucky plates for the Tennessee ones.

"What now?" Tara asked.

"I'm a little tempted to see where this road leads," Owen admitted, peering through the trees to the twisting dirt road ahead.

"You've got to be kidding me."

"I doubt anyone would think to look for us here."

"Where exactly is here?" She leaned forward, as if doing so might somehow reveal more of the road than was currently visible.

"I have no idea."

She shook her head. "I liked your idea of sleeping in the car at a rest area better. At least rest areas have bathrooms and vending machines."

"We have MREs, plus some protein bars and several bottles of water in the survival kit."

"Unless there's a relatively clean bathroom stashed in that kit, my opinion stands."

He sighed. "You used to be more adventurous."

"And you used to be less reckless. When did you change?"

When I realized playing things carefully was getting me nowhere, he thought. *When you met Robert and threw yourself headfirst into a romance with him because he ticked off all the items on your wish list.*

"If you want to go to Virginia and find a rest stop, that's what we'll do. But let's wait here until dark. It'll be easier to escape attention in the dark."

She sighed. "You have a point."

"Don't sound so shocked," he said with a grin.

His echo of her earlier words was enough to earn him a small laugh. "I know I shouldn't be happy you got sucked into my mess, but I'm really glad you're with me. I'm not sure what I would have done if you hadn't been there in that van when I regained consciousness."

He reached across the space between them and brushed a stray twig of hair away from her cheek. "You'd have done what you always do. You'd have come out on top."

Her smile faltered. "I don't feel as if I've come out on top."

"We're not through fighting yet, are we?" He should drop his hand away from her face instead of letting his fingertips linger against her cheek. But with Tara showing no signs of unease, he couldn't bring himself to pull away. He liked the way her skin felt, soft and warm, almost humming with vibrant life.

"I suppose this is a bad time to mention I could use a bathroom break." Tara gave him an apologetic look.

He checked his watch. "Don't suppose you could wait another four hours or so?"

She shook her head.

So much for waiting until after dark to hit the road. "Well, can you wait another hour? I was planning to drive to Abingdon anyway so we could pick up some supplies. We should be there in an hour or so."

"Yeah, I can wait that long."

"If we can find a thrift store, we could stock up on some clothing without making a big dent in our resources," he suggested.

"Good idea. It would be nice to have something that actually fits again." She tugged uncomfortably at her too-tight T-shirt.

He forced his gaze away from her breasts. "I might be able to pick up a laptop computer at a reasonable price, too."

She glanced at him. "Is that a necessity? Five thousand dollars isn't going to last long if we make big purchases."

"I need to be able to stay up on what's happening in the outside world while we're hunkered down."

"Won't you need an internet connection to do that?"

"Yes, but there are ways to do that without being entirely on the grid." He got the SUV turned around on the narrow road and headed for the main road again, hoping the stop hadn't allowed their pursuers to catch up with them. At least they were no longer wearing the Kentucky tags the police would be looking for.

"Do you think we should come up with disguises?" he asked aloud.

"Such as?"

"You could cut your hair. Dye it another color. I could keep growing this beard and buy some gamer glasses—"

"Gamer glasses?"

"Tinted-lens glasses gamers wear to cut down on screen glare. Good for computer users, too. I can probably find some if I can track down a computer store or gamer's store in Abingdon."

"You should buy the hair dye. I'll buy the glasses. In case anyone's paying attention."

"Good thinking." He had reached the main road and he pulled over to a stop, sparing her a quick look before he got back on the blacktop. "So, we find a shopping center. I'll go with you to the computer store to pick out what I need, but you can pay for it. Then we do the opposite when we pick up your hair dye. You pick, I pay."

She flashed a wry grin. "As long as the first place we stop has a bathroom."

"YOU'RE TELLING ME you don't have any sort of security system in your vehicle?" Archer Trask gave Quinn a look of disbelief. "In your line of work?"

"Rather like the doctor who ignores his yearly checkup." Quinn shrugged. "I'm afraid it's a failing many of us have—focusing more on our clients' security needs rather than our own."

Trask didn't appear to believe him, but Quinn didn't care. Trask could prove nothing, and Quinn had access to enough legal help to keep the Bagley County Sheriff's Department from doing any harm.

Meanwhile, he needed to get back to his office and convene a task force to dig deeper into the Tara Bentley case. First line of attack—find out the name of the deputy who'd helped kidnap her and Owen. If he'd been able to get a decent look at the guy himself, he knew Giattina, who'd been parked closer, must have, also. As soon as Quinn finished this pointless interview with Trask, he planned to find Giattina and compare notes. He'd already warned Tony against sharing information with the police that Owen and Tara had revealed while he was acting as their lawyer. Attorney-client privilege was something

Tony took seriously, so Quinn doubted he'd have revealed anything about the suspicious deputy to the investigators interrogating him.

Trask gave Quinn a copy of his statement to sign. "We have your license plate number and the description of your vehicle. We'll find Owen Stiles and Tara Bentley sooner or later." Trask frowned. "If you should hear from them, I'm sure you'll warn them that their decision to flee hardly makes them look innocent."

Quinn signed the statement. "Of course. Am I free to go?"

"You'll let us know if you hear anything from the fugitives?"

"Of course," Quinn lied.

He caught up with Tony Giattina outside, where the lawyer waited by his Mercedes, talking on the phone. His dark eyes met Quinn's, and he said something into the phone, then put it in his pocket. "Would you like to tell me why you're aiding and abetting fugitives?"

Quinn nodded toward the Mercedes. With a sigh, Tony unlocked the car and joined Quinn inside.

"You knew what was going on," Tony said with a grimace. "Is my car bugged?"

Quinn reached under the dashboard and pulled out a small listening device. "I'm sorry. I needed to hear what they had to say to you."

"You breached attorney-client privilege."

"I'm not an attorney."

"No," Tony said with a grimace. "You're a damned spy."

"Former."

"Former, my shiny red—"

"They're in trouble. And I believed them when they told you they recognized one of the Bagley County Sheriff's Department deputies as one of the men who kidnapped them."

"You think the cops were in on what happened to them?"

"Not the whole bunch of them, no. But at least one. And possibly more."

"So why didn't they stick around and identify the guy instead of punching your lights out and running for the hills?"

"Because who would believe them?" Quinn waved at the listening device sitting on the console between them. "You didn't believe them, and you're their lawyer."

Tony fell silent a moment. "What do you expect from me?"

"Your silence. They told you about the kidnapper as part of your attorney-client relationship. It remains privileged until such time as they give you permission to reveal it."

"You don't want me to tell what I know? If you and my clients are right, there's a kidnapper working as a Bagley County deputy, and you want that information kept silent?"

"I do."

Tony shook his head. "That makes no damn sense."

Quinn reached for the listening device and slipped it into his pocket. "What do you think would happen if we told what we know? Let's say Trask believes us. He'd track down the deputy you saw, get your identification of the man and start questioning him. Which would be a disaster."

"Why would it be a disaster?"

"Because I've come to believe the people behind Tara Bentley's kidnapping are up to something far more dangerous than a simple abduction. And if we tip our hand, we may not find out what their plan is until it's much too late."

Chapter Nine

"Wow. Is that you?"

Tara looked up at the sound of Owen's voice, but it took a moment to realize that the gangly hipster in the saggy gray beanie shuffling toward her was her best friend. The cap looked ancient and well used, and it went well with the rest of his slouchy attire, from the baggy faded jeans to the oversize navy hoodie with the name of an obscure eighties' metal band on the front. The sleek design of his amber-lensed glasses should have looked out of sync with the rest of his slacker aesthetic, but somehow the glasses seemed perfectly at home perched on his long, thin nose.

"I almost didn't recognize you," she said as he set a large shopping bag from an electronics store on the hood of the SUV.

"Likewise." He waved his hand toward her hair. "I like the purple."

She patted her now-short hair self-consciously. The budget hair salon in the Abingdon shopping center had done a decent job giving her a spiky gamine cut, but the spray-on color she'd added was way outside her normal comfort zone.

"We need to hit the road, but I had an idea for the SUV." Owen pulled a small bag from inside his jacket and reached inside, withdrawing a small stack of bumper stickers. "Start sticking them on the back of the SUV."

The stickers, she saw, embraced every social justice issue known to man, including some that contradicted each other.

"It would be better if this were a Volkswagen Beetle," she muttered when he rejoined her at the back of the SUV after he'd stashed his new computer inside.

"You make do with what you have," Owen said with a shrug. "The main thing is, it doesn't look like the SUV that left Kentucky this morning."

She tugged at the ends of her hair. "And we don't look like the people who left Kentucky this morning."

"Exactly." He cocked his head. "Don't suppose you could get your nose pierced?"

She gave his arm a light slap. "No."

"Maybe your belly button?"

"Get in the car."

From Abingdon, they took I-81 north, heading for the next rest stop. Spotting a sign for a sub shop at one of the interstate exits just south of the rest area, Owen pulled off the highway to grab a couple of sandwiches for their dinner.

By the time they finally reached the rest stop, the afternoon had started fading into twilight. Owen found a parking place a few spaces away from the nearest car and parked.

"Home, sweet home," he murmured.

"Let's take a restroom break," Tara suggested. "Give me a couple of dollars and I'll buy some drinks to go with our dinner."

The bathrooms were blessedly clean and human traffic at the rest stop was just busy enough for Owen and Tara to be able to blend in without any trouble. She bought the drinks and, while she was there, picked up a few of the brochures for south Virginia campgrounds and attractions.

She showed Owen one of the brochures over dinner. "It's a campground about two hours east of here. We pay a small fee for a campsite. There's a communal restroom within walking distance, and a charging station for electronics. They even advertise free Wi-Fi."

Owen looked at the brochure, his brow furrowed. "There is a tent stashed in the back of the SUV..."

"We stay here tonight, and then tomorrow we can settle in there. Maybe you can put that computer you bought to use."

"HOW'S THE SALMON?" Becky Cameron asked.

"Delicious." Quinn tried to remain expressionless, not sure he was ready to let his colleague know that her sudden desire to socialize was beginning to make him uneasy. He turned keeping people at arm's length into an art form. Becky knew that better than most, having worked with him off and on for more than fifteen years.

"Are you ever going to tell me about your adventure this morning?" she asked, delicately picking at her own pan-seared trout.

"Not much to tell."

She gestured with one long-fingered, graceful hand toward the bruise shadowing his jawline. "Owen Stiles packs a nice punch."

"We taught him well."

"You don't seem particularly incensed at the idea of having your vehicle stolen by a trusted employee."

"Life is full of surprises."

Becky smiled, showing a flash of straight white teeth. "Subject dropped."

"That's for the best," he agreed, glancing around the crowded restaurant. "For the here and now, at least."

She nodded, taking a dainty bite of the trout. "We can catch up at work in the morning."

A few minutes of thick silence stretched between them before Becky spoke again. "You're wondering why I invited you here when I know as well as you do that there are certain topics we can't discuss in public."

"The question did cross my mind."

Becky's smile was full of sympathy. "I don't mean to be so enigmatic. That's your bailiwick."

He managed a smile. "But you clearly brought me here for a reason."

"Socializing isn't reason enough?"

He quirked one eyebrow, making her smile.

"Right," she said, the smile fading. "I wanted to talk to you about something not connected to work. And I was afraid if I tried to approach you at the office, I would lose my nerve."

Now he was intrigued. "I can't imagine you ever losing your nerve, Becky. About anything."

"It's about Mitch."

Suddenly, the half filet of salmon he'd eaten felt like a lump of lead in his stomach. He laid down his fork and took a drink of water to cover his sudden discomfort. "Has something changed?"

"Maybe." A furrow creased her brow. "There's some indication that he might not have died in the helicopter crash in Tablis."

Quinn froze in the act of straightening his napkin across his lap. "I saw the crash myself. We searched the area thoroughly for over a week. Men under my watch died trying to recover all the bodies. But it was the rainy season, and the current in the river where they crashed was brutally swift. Several bodies washed downriver and were never recovered."

"I saw film of the crash. I know how unlikely it is that he survived."

Quinn reached across the table and covered her hand with his. "I know you want to believe there's a chance he survived."

"I don't know what I want to believe, Quinn. It's been nearly ten years. If he survived, why didn't he try to reach someone? I know it's grasping at straws. It's just—what if he's out there? Maybe he doesn't remember what happened or who he is. Maybe he just needs to see a familiar face to trigger the rest of his memories."

He gave her hand another squeeze before letting go. "I don't think it works that way. But if you want me to put out some feelers with some of my old contacts in Kaziristan—"

"I'd appreciate it," she said with a grateful smile. She looked down at her plate. "I don't know about you, but I think my appetite is gone."

"You want to get out of here? Maybe we could

head back to the office and talk about the subject we were supposed to talk about?"

She nodded. "You go ahead. I'll get the check and meet you there."

"I can wait," he said, feeling an unexpected protectiveness of her. He'd never thought of Becky as someone who needed anyone or anything. Even her relationship with Mitch Talbot, a marine colonel she'd met when she was stationed at the US embassy in Tablis, Kaziristan, had seemed lopsided. She was the diplomat, a woman of culture, education and power, while he was a gruff leatherneck more at home in fatigues leading his men into combat.

But clearly, she'd loved him deeply if she was willing to put her reputation and her connections on the line to find him ten years after his presumed death. Was she setting herself up for a fresh new heartbreak?

She was obviously going to look for the man, whether Quinn helped her or not. And even though the thought of trying to dig up those old bones made him positively queasy, it was the least he owed her.

After all, he was the man who'd sent Mitch Talbot to his death.

MORNING WAS JUST a hint of pink promise in the eastern sky when Owen woke from a restless sleep. At bedtime the night before, he and Tara had tried to sleep on the narrow bench seats, but after the second time Tara tumbled off the seat into the floorboard, they decided it made more sense to fold down the seats and use the now-flat cargo area to deploy the sleeping bags stashed among other survival gear in the underfloor storage area of the SUV. Given the dropping temperature outside, they decided to zip the two bags into one spacious double bag. Curling up back to back, they'd fallen asleep in relative warmth, if not comfort.

At some point during the night, however, they'd ended up face-to-face, their limbs entangled beneath the down-filled cover of the sleeping bags.

For a heady moment, Owen wanted nothing more than to stay right where he was for the rest of his life, his skin against hers, her warmth enfolding him with a sense of sublime rightness he had never felt with anyone but her.

It would be so much easier if he could have found that feeling of completion with another woman. He'd tried more than once over the years to move on, to seek a relationship, a life, where Tara Bentley wasn't the most important part of it. It had taken a long time for him to come to terms with the fact that as long as Tara was in his life, she would always be the most important part of it.

Which meant the only way to move on with his life would be to let her go completely.

He gently extricated himself from her sleeping embrace. She made a soft groaning noise that echoed inside his own chest, but he forced himself to keep moving rather than return to the warmth of her body. Trying not to wake her, he unzipped his side of the sleeping back, wincing at the rush of cold outside its down-filled insulation. He grabbed his jacket from the front seat and added it to the sweatshirt and jeans he'd worn last night for warmth before he opened the door and stepped out into the chilly morning air.

Across the rest area parking lot, a handful of other travelers were up and moving, taking advantage of the bathrooms and vending machines. One machine seemed to dispense hot coffee, he noticed, swirls of steam rising from cups held by weary travelers exiting the building.

He pulled up the collar of his jacket and tugged the ratty beanie over his head, grimacing at the need for disguise. It was too dark for the glasses, so he left them in his jacket pocket as he slouched his way across to the rest area center.

After a quick bathroom break, the siren song of coffee drew him to the vending machine. He bought a couple of cups and tucked them to his chest under one arm while he studied the vending machine selections. Sweet or salty? Tara wasn't much of a breakfast person, but they couldn't be sure when they'd be able to eat again, so she needed something with some protein. A bag of peanuts and a pack of cheese crackers would have to do.

He didn't immediately notice a new arrival at the rest area center, so it was with a flutter of shock that he turned away from the vending machine to find a Virginia State Police officer standing only a couple of yards away.

He froze at first, his heart beating a tattoo against his ribs. Coffee sloshed in the cups pressed against his chest, almost spilling down his shirt.

Turning as slowly as he dared, he settled the cups and edged toward the side of the room, where a few travelers were looking through the brochure racks advertising local tourist stops.

He glanced back toward the policeman. He seemed to be looking for something.

Or someone?

Owen edged toward the door with his purchases, hoping he wouldn't do something stupid like trip over his own feet and draw attention toward himself. Tara was asleep in the SUV, with no idea how close they were to being discovered.

One foot in front of the other...

"Excuse me, sir? Have you seen this woman?" The voice, so close, made him jerk with surprise. Some of the coffee spilled onto the pavement in front of the rest-area door.

Slowly, he turned to face the policeman. The man was holding a printed flyer with a woman's photograph on it. Owen nearly melted with relief when he realized the woman on the flyer wasn't Tara.

"I'm sorry, no," he said, faking a midwestern accent. "Just driving through."

"If you see anything, give us a call." The policeman started to hand Owen a card, then belatedly realized his hands were full. He slipped the card into the pocket of Owen's jacket. "Have a safe trip."

"Thanks." Owen gave a nod and headed quickly across the parking lot to the SUV.

Tara was awake when he opened the door. He set the coffee and snacks on the floorboard and glanced over his shoulder. The policeman had remained outside the rest area center, talking to travelers as they entered and exited the place.

Following his gaze, Tara asked with alarm, "Is that a cop?"

"He seems to be looking for a missing woman. I nearly had a heart attack when he stopped me to ask if I'd seen her."

"Do you think he recognized you?"

"He didn't seem to." He looked at Tara. "Stop staring at him. He'll think we're up to something."

"We *are* up to something. Sort of." Tara forced her gaze away from the policeman, letting it settle on Owen's vending-machine bounty. "Coffee. Thank goodness."

"You need to eat something, too. I bought you some peanuts for protein."

"Yes, Mom." She tore open the packet of peanuts. "Want some?"

Owen's appetite was gone. Even the coffee, which he'd been craving just a little while ago, seemed entirely unappetizing. "Go ahead. I'll worry about getting us ready to get back on the road."

They'd filled the gas tank back in Abingdon, so they were good for several more miles before they'd have to worry about stopping for fuel. The tires looked fine, and all of the SUV's gauges were reading in the normal range. He settled in the driver's seat, his nerves finally steady enough for him to sit still without fidgeting.

"I think enough time has passed now that we can leave without looking as if we're running away," he said, glancing over his shoulder at Tara.

She licked salt off her fingertips and looked back at him. "Even though that's what we're doing."

"You have a better idea?"

She shook her head. "Let's get out of here."

"You can stay in the back and get a little more sleep if you want."

"No, I'm wide awake. Hold on and I'll come up front." She exited the back door and climbed into the front, first putting Owen's cooling cup of coffee in the console's cup holder. "You should drink that before it gets cold."

He looked at it and shook his head. "You can have it if you want."

She climbed into the passenger seat and buckled in, then picked up the cup. "If you insist."

They fell silent until they were well clear of the rest area and moving east on I-81. As they passed through the scenic town of Rural Retreat, Tara set down her empty coffee cup and turned in her seat to look at him.

"Maybe we should call your boss," she suggested.

"I'm not sure it's safe."

"Is it that? Or is it that you don't want to ask for help."

He angled a quick look at her. She gazed back at him, a knowing look in her eyes that made him feel completely exposed.

"I know you don't like asking for help," she added, her tone gentler. "I know why."

"I'm not afraid to call Quinn if we need him."

"But you're afraid if you call him now, he'll see you as weak. Just like your father used to accuse you of being."

He pressed his lips to a thin line, annoyed. "Not every decision I make in my life is influenced by what my father said to me when I was fifteen."

"Then call Quinn. He told you to get in touch, right?"

"Yes, but—"

"No buts." She pulled the cell phone from the caddy at the front of the console, where it had been charging all night. "Call him."

"I'm driving."

"I'll dial. Just tell me the number."

With a sigh, he gave her the number of Quinn's business cell phone. "It's still awfully early," he warned.

"Didn't you once tell me you think Quinn never sleeps?" She put the phone on speaker and dialed the number.

Quinn answered on the first ring, "Don't tell me anything about where you are. Just tell me if you're all right."

"We're fine," Owen answered, surprised at the relief that flooded him at the sound of his boss's voice. He wasn't close to Quinn at all, having barely spoken to the man more than a dozen times since he took the job at Campbell Cove Security. But just knowing he had someone besides Tara out there, trying to watch his back, was enough to bolster his sagging spirits. "We've disguised ourselves and the vehicle, so we're trying to find somewhere to hunker down until we can formulate a plan for our next steps."

"I think your next steps should include trying to figure out who wants the information Tara has in her head that they can't find anywhere else."

"That's where you could give us some help," Tara interjected. "I know what information they're looking for, but I'm not in the know about which groups might be looking for that information. Do you have a dossier on the groups most likely to be trying to make a big show of force at the symposium?"

"That's going to be a lot of dossiers," he warned.

"What about the deputy we saw? Maybe if we could get an ID on him, we could dig deeper and figure out who he associates with," Owen suggested.

"On it. The Bagley County Sheriff's Department inconveniently doesn't have a website, but Archer Trask has cooperated with us on a previous case he was investigating, so I'm going to see if I can exploit that relationship to get information without raising his suspicions."

"You're going to try to outcop a cop?" Tara asked skeptically.

"We have our ways." There was a hint of amusement in Quinn's voice. "I'll handle that end of things. Meanwhile, you need to stay off the grid as much as you can. You found the cash and all the supplies?"

"We did," Owen answered.

"You're a scary man, Alexander Quinn," Tara added.

"I like to be prepared," he said. "Call again in four hours. If everything is good, tell me that it's not. If you're in trouble, say everything is okay. Understood?"

Owen exchanged glances with Tara. Both her eyebrows were near her hairline, but she said, "Understood."

Quinn ended the call without another word, and she put the phone back in the console holder.

"So," she said, "where exactly do we plan to hunker down?"

"I think we need to find that campsite I was telling you about. And fast."

The sooner they were off the road, the less likely it was that someone would spot their

SUV and start wondering if it might be the missing vehicle from Kentucky with the two fugitives inside.

Chapter Ten

"I can't believe you bought marshmallows."

Tara looked up from the shopping bag she was unpacking to find Owen holding a bag of the puffy white sweets. "I don't go camping without marshmallows. Or hot dogs," she added, pulling a pack of wieners from the shopping bag.

Owen sighed, but she saw the hint of a smile cross his face. "I hope you got mustard, too."

She waggled the mustard bottle at him. "And ketchup for me."

He made a face. "I appreciate the fact that you're trying to make this a fun experience—"

"I'm trying to get through this without losing my sanity," she corrected, her voice rising with a rush of emotion. "If I treat this like one of our nights out camping at Kingdom Come State Park, maybe I can get through this thing without being institutionalized."

Silence fell between them for a long, tense moment before Owen finally spoke. "I'm sorry."

She shook her head. "You have nothing to be sorry for. You're in this mess, too, and it's all because of me."

"No, I meant I'm sorry about Robert. I haven't really said that to you. I know you loved him, even if you didn't love him enough to go through with the wedding. And you haven't really had a moment to yourself to just grieve."

"I don't have time to grieve. I have to figure out this whole mess. It's about me and what I know. It's my responsibility."

He stood up from where he crouched by the fire pit he was building and crossed to where she stood by the SUV. He cupped her face between his hands, and emotion surged in her chest, making her feel as if she were about to explode. She tamped down the feelings roiling through her and forced herself to meet his soft-eyed gaze.

"You don't have to do this alone. Any of it."

Blinking back tears she didn't want to spill, she managed a smile. "I know you're on my side. You always are."

Something flickered in his gaze, an emotion she couldn't quite read, and he dropped his hands from her face and stepped a couple of feet away. "I'll put the hot dogs in the cooler." He picked up the pack of wieners and walked back to the campsite.

Even though he was only a few feet away from her, she suddenly felt as if she were alone, cut off from anything and anyone important to her. It was a hollow, terrible feeling.

She shook off the sensation. She wasn't alone. She hadn't been alone since the sixth grade, when Owen Stiles had literally stumbled into her life, dropping his lunch tray at her feet and soiling her favorite pair of Chuck Taylors. Once she got past the desire to strangle him, she'd found a friend who'd never, ever failed her.

He wouldn't fail her now. If there was anything in her life that was constant and permanent, it was Owen Stiles. His friendship was everything to her, which was why she'd fight anyone and anything, including her own libido, to keep him in her life.

While she was picking up camping supplies at a store in the nearby town of Weatherly, Owen had been busy setting up camp. The tent he'd found stored in the SUV now stood next to the campfire. It was larger than she'd expected, but still cozy enough that they should be able to stay warm in the night.

"Did you find any nightcrawlers?" he asked as she crossed with the rest of the supplies to where he crouched by the fire pit.

"Of course. No grocery store this close to a campground would be caught dead without a bait shop section." She sat cross-legged on the ground next to him and dug in her grocery bag until she retrieved two small plastic bowls full of dirt. There were little pinprick holes in the plastic lid of the containers. "Here. Have some worms."

"There's a curve of the river that runs near here, according to the online map." He pulled the cell phone from his pocket and waggled it at her, a smile flirting with his lips. "I don't know how Daniel Boone made it across the wilderness without Google."

A gust of wind lifted Tara's short locks and rustled the grocery bag. She looked up through the trees to discover that the sunny sky that had greeted them earlier that morning was gone, swallowed by slate-colored clouds scudding along with the wind.

"I don't think we're going to get to have marshmallows or hot dogs tonight," she said with a heavy sigh. "I bought a few cans of soup, though. I think we could probably heat one up using the camp stove before the rain hits."

"You're being a good sport about this," Owen commented as he gathered up the supplies he'd laid out on the ground by their would-be campfire. "I know how you like your creature comforts."

"It's not like this is your mess, Owen. You didn't drag me into this. It's the other way around."

"I dragged myself into it."

"Trying to help me."

"You'd have done the same." He finished stowing away the equipment in the waterproof duffel and stuffed it into the tent, leaving out only the portable camp stove and a small saucepan. He looked up at the sky. "We probably have another fifteen minutes before the bottom falls out of the sky, so what kind of soup do we have there?"

She pulled out three cans. "Chicken noodle, vegetable and beef, and chicken-corn chowder."

"The chowder sounds good. Filling."

She put the other two cans back in the shopping bag and pulled the tab ring on the can of chowder. It opened with a quiet snick. "Hope there aren't any bears nearby."

"Me, too." Owen added the butane canister to the camp stove and turned the knob until it clicked and a flame appeared at the center of the burner. "Oh, look, it works."

"You weren't sure it would?" Tara asked.

"I hoped it would." He set the saucepan on the burner and reached out for the can of soup.

Tara handed it to him and crouched beside him. "I didn't think to buy any paper bowls."

"There are plastic bowls and eating utensils in the duffel bag."

She retrieved them and sat down beside Owen in front of the stove. "I still think your boss is some sort of madman, but at least he's a madman who knows how to prepare for any eventuality."

"I imagine he learned about being prepared the hard way. I've heard some stories—all told in hushed tones, of course—about some of his adventures during his time in the CIA."

"Do you believe them?"

"Most of them, yeah. You don't get the kind of reputation Quinn has if you spent your years in the CIA behind some cushy desk in an embassy."

The advent of the clouds overhead had driven out most of the warmth of the day, and there was a definite damp chill in the increasing wind. Tara edged closer to Owen, glad for his body heat and the warmth drifting toward her from the camp stove. The soup was already starting to burble in the pan.

"Maybe we should eat inside the tent," she suggested. "I think it's going to rain any minute."

He looked up at the sky. "Good idea. Here, hand me the bowls and I'll spoon this up. Then you can take the food inside and I'll clean up out here."

Tara took the bowls of soup Owen handed to

her and ducked inside the tent. Their sleeping bags covered most of the tent floor; as they had the night before, they'd zipped the bags together in order to take advantage of each other's body heat. With the sudden dip in the temperature, Tara had a feeling it was going to be a damp, chilly night.

Owen appeared through the flap of the tent, carrying the extinguished stove and the cleaned-up cooking pot. He left the stove just inside the tent to cool but stowed away the cooking pot, then took his food from Tara. He nodded at her untouched bowl. "Eat up before it gets cold."

She took a bite of the hearty chowder. It was pretty good for canned soup. "I don't suppose Quinn has sent you the dossiers we asked for."

Owen pulled the burner phone from his pocket. "To be honest, I haven't checked. I was keeping the phone off to conserve the battery, since I don't want to risk putting any sort of drain on the SUV's engine until we're on the road again."

They had agreed not to camp too close to the campground amenities, wanting to avoid interaction with other campers. The restrooms were only a hundred yards away, hidden by the woods, but the office was another hundred yards away, which meant the charging stations available to campers were also that far away.

"I'm getting a Wi-Fi signal from the camp-ground. It's not the strongest, but it's better than nothing."

"Think it'll be strong enough for a file to download?"

"There's an email trying to download. It's slow going, but I'll bet it's from Quinn. Nobody else would have the email for this phone." He stuck the phone back in his pocket. "Let's finish eating. I'll check again when we're finished. Maybe it'll have downloaded by then."

Tara suddenly felt anything but hungry, but she forced herself to eat. If they were going to be running for their lives over the next few days, she needed her strength. Food wasn't a luxury. It was a necessity.

She managed to remain patient until her bowl was empty. She set it aside and looked up at Owen. "Can you check the email again?"

He gave her a sympathetic look and pulled out his phone. "Looks as if it's finished. Let's see what we've got."

She scooted closer so she could see the phone screen. The file attached to the email appeared to be a portable document file. Owen clicked the pdf file and a summary page appeared. Tara scanned the words, which informed them that the following files contained background details on the employees of Security Solutions. According to Quinn's notes, he was also trying to come up with potential connections between the sheriff's department and Security Solutions along with trying to connect members of the sheriff's department to any of the known terror groups who had both the motive and the means to stage a significant terror event on American soil.

"What do you expect to find in these dossiers?" Owen asked.

"Connections," she answered. "I'm thinking it would have to be someone who's in a position to take any of the information I might have supplied to the kidnappers and do something with it."

"Who might that be?"

"Well, obviously, my bosses, but since they already have the information I have, they wouldn't need to bother with a kidnapping."

"Do you have an assistant?"

"Yes, but Karen wouldn't be next in line for the job if I suddenly disappear."

"But could she use the information you have if she could get her hands on it?"

Tara thought about it. "Theoretically, anyone could. But it's likely that by now, my bosses have already changed all the details of the event. Either postponed it or moved venues."

"So maybe you're not in danger anymore."

The same thought had just occurred to her. "Maybe. But why do I still feel as if I'm in danger?"

"I think maybe because Alexander Quinn thinks you still are, and if he does, he must have a reason." Owen set aside his empty soup bowl and pulled the burner phone out of his pocket. "Let's find out why."

"Will he answer?" she asked as he dialed the number.

"He'd better."

Tara scooted closer so she could hear the other end of the call. The phone rang twice before a drawling voice answered, "Roy's Auto Repair."

"I'm calling about my green Cutlass GT," Owen said, arching his eyebrows at Tara.

"I'll check, sir." After a brief pause, the voice on the other line continued. "Still checking, but Roy told me to ask how you're doing today."

"Just lousy," Owen answered.

"Sorry to hear that." The voice on the other end of the line suddenly sounded like Quinn. "Thought I said I'd call you."

"You did. But we have a question."

"Shoot."

"Why exactly do you think Tara is still in danger, when you have to know her bosses have already changed the details of the project?"

SHEFFIELD TAVERN WAS less a bar and more a restaurant that happened to serve liquor at a bar in the back. On this Monday afternoon, the bar crowd was laid-back and sparse, though it would probably pick up later in the evening.

Archer Trask had agreed to meet Maddox Heller for an early dinner at the tavern more out of curiosity than any real desire to deal with the Campbell Cove Security agent, given the way his previous day had gone. But the chance that Heller might provide some needed information about what, exactly, had sent Tara Bentley and Owen Stiles on the run again was worth putting up with bar food and average beer.

To his surprise, Heller brought his wife, Iris, a tall, slim woman with wavy black hair and coffee-brown eyes. She smiled at Trask, extending her hand as Heller introduced them.

As Trask shook Iris's hand, he felt an odd tingle in his hand, almost as if static electricity had sparked between them. But if Iris noticed, she didn't show it.

Trask took a seat across the table from Heller and his pretty wife, looking curiously from one to the other. "I'm wondering why you asked me to meet you here."

"Alexander Quinn requested that I contact you about something that's arisen in the Robert Mallory murder case," Heller said. "He's on other business, or he'd have asked to speak with you himself."

Something about this meeting didn't quite feel right, but Trask decided to play along as if he weren't suspicious. "Not sure there's much point talking to y'all, considering you weren't there."

"Actually, there is." Heller bent down and picked up the worn leather satchel he'd brought with him to the tavern. He unbuckled the latch and flipped the satchel cover open. "You see, my wife, among her many other talents, is an artist. And we've begun to use her talent in some of our cases where we work with witnesses—"

"She's a sketch artist, you mean," Trask interrupted, beginning to lose his patience. His day had been long already, and the rest of the week stretched out in front of him like a series of endless frustrations and dead ends. "But unless she saw who shot Robert Mallory, I don't see how she can help us."

"Has anyone told you what Tara Bentley says happened to her the day of her wedding?"

Trask tried not to show his sudden spark of interest, but he couldn't help sitting up a little straighter. "No. I assume she and her partner in crime told their lawyer something about their disappearance, but he invoked the lawyer-client privilege thing, so we're still in the dark. Damn inconvenient, that. Kind of makes it hard to do my job, you know?"

"She was kidnapped," Heller said bluntly. "Two men in a white cargo van. Owen Stiles happened upon them in the middle of it and was knocked out and thrown into the van, as well."

Trask stared at him in disbelief. "You've got to be kidding me."

"Yeah, that was about the reaction Owen and Tara were expecting," Heller drawled, looking so disappointed that Trask started feeling a little guilty for his instant reaction.

Then he got angry about feeling guilty. "It's a ridiculous story. Did they happen to tell you why someone would kidnap a bride on her wedding day when, oh, by the way, the groom ended up facedown in his own blood in the groom's room?"

"They don't know why. That's part of the problem."

"How did they get away?"

"Their captors miscalculated when they bound Tara's hands. They bound them in front of her with duct tape rather than behind her, and she was able to undo the tape around Owen's hands. He freed her, and that gave them time to prepare for a blitz attack on their captors when they stopped and opened the doors to transfer them wherever they were planning to take them."

"What then?" Trask asked, glancing at Heller's wife to see how she was reacting to the story Heller was telling. She had a placid look in her eyes, tinged by a hint of jaded knowing that suggested she'd seen and heard far stranger things in her life.

"They were able to get away, although the kidnappers pursued them in the woods for a while. Finally, the kidnappers retreated, and Tara and Owen found an old abandoned cabin for shelter from the rain that night."

"What then?"

"They got in touch with us, and we got them a lawyer. You know the rest." Heller's expression was completely neutral, which in his case was a tell. There was a little more to the story about how Bentley and Stiles got from point A to point B, but Heller wasn't going to share. Trask supposed in the long run, it wasn't that big a deal. What he really wanted to know was why they changed their minds about turning themselves in.

"They decided against turning themselves in while they were right outside the police department," Trask said. "Why?"

"Because yesterday morning, when they

showed up to turn themselves in, they spotted one of the men who kidnapped them entering the sheriff's department, dressed in a deputy's uniform. Alexander Quinn saw the man, too, and he described him in detail to Iris. She made this sketch." Heller pulled a sheet of paper out of his satchel and laid it on the table in front of Trask.

Trask looked at the sketch. It was extremely well drawn, full of details and nuance. He recognized the face immediately.

"You know him, don't you?" Heller asked, his tone urgent.

Trask looked up at Heller, too stunned to hide his reaction. "Yes, I do."

"Who is he?"

Trask shoved the sketch back across the table, his stomach roiling. "This is bull. Just like the story Bentley and Stiles shoveled your way."

"Who is the man in the sketch?" Heller persisted.

"Maddox," Iris said in a warning tone, clutching his arm.

Something passed between Heller and his wife, and the man's bulldog demeanor softened. When he spoke again, his voice was gentle with a hint of sympathetic understanding. "You obviously recognize the man. Even if the story Tara and Owen told is bull, like you think, there must be a reason they chose this man as the scape-goat. Who is he?"

"He's my brother," Trask growled, his stomach starting to ache. "All right? He's my brother."

Chapter Eleven

The long pause on the other end of the line only convinced Owen that he and Tara were right. Quinn had his own agenda, as always. He and Tara might be valuable pawns in this particular chess game, but pawns they were, nevertheless.

"It doesn't matter whether or not her bosses have changed the details of the project," Quinn said finally. "What matters is letting your opponent continue to believe you're better armed than he is."

"What does that even mean?" Owen asked, trying not to lose his temper. Getting angry wouldn't get him any closer to uncovering Quinn's motives.

Tara put her hand on Owen's arm. "It means Mr. Quinn wants the people who kidnapped me to think there's a reason I'm not rushing back to civilization with my story."

"There is a reason. One of the guys who kidnapped us is working for the cops."

"They'll be wondering what information we're trying to protect by keeping you hidden," Quinn explained. "They'll want to know what that information might be, and they'll take risks to find out."

"But how does that help us if we don't know who they are?" Tara asked.

"We know who one of them is," Quinn corrected after a brief pause. "I just got a message from Maddox Heller. I don't believe you know this, but his wife is working for us as a freelance sketch artist. I gave her the description of the deputy you say kidnapped the two of you."

"You saw him?" Tara asked.

"Yes."

"Unbelievable," Owen muttered. "I barely got a glimpse of him myself. How did you get a good enough look to give anyone a description?"

"Close observation is what I do. It's what I've done for decades now." Quinn's tone was abrupt. "The point is, Heller showed Archer Trask the sketch Iris made, and now we have an ID on the man who kidnapped you."

"Who is he?" Owen asked.

"He's Virgil Trask. Archer Trask's older brother."

"Trask identified him?" Tara looked at Owen, her eyes wide.

"Reluctantly, according to Heller. I haven't briefed him yet. He left a text for me on my other phone."

"Unbelievable," Tara muttered. "The kidnapper is the brother of the cop trying to bring us in."

"This could end up working in our favor," Quinn said. "Their relationship is going to force Trask to either play this investigation strictly by the book or risk being accused of a cover-up. He knows it, and he knows we know it, too."

"But is he going to take seriously the possibility that his brother is involved with a terrorist plot?" Owen asked.

"It doesn't matter. He knows *we're* taking it seriously, and we have the clout to make waves if he doesn't at least explore the possibility."

Tara shook her head. "What if he takes himself off the case? Won't that be the protocol if his brother is now a suspect?"

"If it were a large department, yes. But the Bagley County Sheriff's Department has only three investigators, and one of those is on maternity leave. The other one is Virgil Trask."

"Great. He's an investigator, too?"

"We're on top of this." Quinn's tone was firm and, if Owen was reading him correctly, impatient. "I'll call back before ten. You continue lying low." He ended the call abruptly.

"Your boss is a sweetheart, isn't he?" Tara's tone was bone dry.

Owen looked at the phone display. The battery was getting low. He dug in Quinn's duffel for one of the portable chargers Quinn had packed. As he plugged in the phone to charge, he looked up at Tara, waving the portable charger in front of him. "This is why we need to trust him. He's always prepared. He's always a step ahead of whatever problem he faces."

"You make him sound like a superhero."

"No, just a man who's seen the worst the world has to offer and knows what it takes to face it." Owen pushed the phone aside and shifted position until he was face-to-face with Tara, their knees touching. The sense of déjà vu made him smile. "Remember the last time we shared a tent like this?"

The tension lines in Tara's face relaxed. A smile played on her lips. "The summer before we started high school. We sat just like this in the tent and swore we'd be friends forever."

He smiled back at her. "High school should have posed a problem for us. You, the cute little cheerleader with all the popular boys in love with you, and me, the socially awkward computer geek…"

She reached across the space between them

and took his hand. "You, the brilliant, funny, kindhearted friend who never, ever let me down."

He twined his fingers through hers, his pulse picking up speed until he could hear it thundering in his ears, nearly eclipsing the steady syncopation of rain on top of the tent. "Then why do you think I'll let you down if things change between us?"

She stared at him in shock, as if he'd just reached across the space between them and slapped her. She pulled her hand back from his. "You know how I feel about this."

"I know you're afraid of things changing between us."

"You should be, too." She had turned away from him and now sat with her shoulders hunched. "I don't know what I'd do without you."

"You wouldn't be without me. Don't you see that? You'd just be with me in a different way. A deeper way."

She shot a glare at him over her shoulder. "You don't know that's how it would go. What if we discovered we weren't good together that way?" She shook her head fiercely. "I can't risk that."

Owen didn't push her. It would be useless when she had so clearly closed her mind to the idea that they could have something more than just friendship.

He pulled his jacket on like armor, protecting himself against both the dropping temperature outside and the distinct chill that had grown inside the tent with his tentative attempt to address the ongoing sexual tension between them.

But he didn't know how much longer he could keep denying what he felt for her. Maybe she was happy living this half life, but he was all too quickly reaching the point where something had to give.

ARCHER TRASK POURED himself two fingers of Maker's Mark bourbon and stared at the amber liquor with an ache in his soul. It would be one thing if he could just laugh off the allegation against Virgil with full assurance, but he couldn't really do that, could he? Virgil might be wearing a badge now, but he'd spent most of his youth caught up in one mess or another.

Their father's money had spared him the worst consequences of his reckless spirit, but even after Virgil left behind his teenage years, there had been whispers of questionable behavior, hadn't there? Complaints from prisoners of rough treatment. A tendency to rub some of his fellow deputies the wrong way.

But getting involved in a kidnapping?

Archer swirled the bourbon around in the tumbler, his mouth feeling suddenly parched.

Just a sip wouldn't hurt. A sip and the burn of the whiskey to drive away the chill that seemed to seep right through to his bones.

But as one of the sheriff's department's three investigators, he was always on call, especially with Tammy Sloan out on maternity leave. He couldn't afford to show up on a call with liquor on his breath.

He pushed the glass away and picked up his cell phone. Virgil's number wasn't exactly first on his speed dial. In fact, as brothers, they weren't much alike at all. Trask had always chalked that fact up to having different mothers—his father's first wife had died suddenly of an aneurysm when Virgil was a small boy. Maybe that loss so early in his life had led to his wild ways when he reached adolescence. Or maybe Virgil had just been one of those people who could only learn by making his own mistakes.

Trask pushed the number for his brother and waited for Virgil to answer. Three rings later, Virgil's gravelly voice rumbled across the line. "What's up, Archie?"

Trask gritted his teeth at the nickname. "Just haven't talked to you in a while. We always seem to miss each other at work."

"You can thank Tammy Sloan for that. Squeezing out another kid and leaving us to pick up her slack."

"What are you working on these days?"

"Car theft ring over in Campbell Cove, mostly. You've got that rich kid's murder, don't you?"

"Yeah. Wonder why you didn't catch that call? You're senior in rank."

"I was off that weekend. Out of town."

"Yeah? Where'd you go?"

"Camping up near Kingdom Come. Me and Ty Miller. Thought we'd see if we could pull a few rainbow trout out of Looney Creek, but we got skunked."

"Rainbows won't be stocked in Looney Creek for another month."

"Reckon that's why we got skunked." Virgil laughed. "Why the sudden interest in my itinerary?"

"Just wondering why you weren't the one called to the church. It's turning out to be a real puzzle."

"So I hear. Grapevine says the girl and her boy on the side nearly turned themselves in to you yesterday morning but something spooked them away. Any idea what?"

"No," Trask lied, his stomach aching. "Not a clue."

"If you need a little help, let me know. This car theft ring ain't going anywhere anytime soon, and I could spare some time for my little brother."

"I'll keep that in mind." Trask realized he was gripping his phone so hard his fingers were starting to hurt. He loosened his grip and added, "We should meet up for lunch soon. Catch up with each other."

"Sounds like a real good idea. I'll call you tomorrow and we'll set up a time. Listen, I hate to rush you off the phone, but I've got some catch-up paperwork to do—"

"Understood. Talk to you tomorrow." Trask hung up the phone and stared at the glimmering amber liquid in the tumbler still sitting in front of him.

Just one sip wouldn't hurt, would it?

He shoved himself up from the table and grabbed the tumbler. At the sink, he poured the glass of whiskey down the drain. The fumes rising from the drain smelled vaguely of charred oak and caramel.

He wasn't sure what his brother had been doing the day of Robert Mallory's murder, but he was pretty sure Virgil was lying about going camping with Ty Miller up near Kingdom Come State Park.

The question was, why was he lying? To give himself an alibi for something? Or to give an alibi to Ty Miller, his longtime best friend and former partner in crime?

One way or another, Trask had to find out

where Virgil had really been the day of the Mallory murder.

No matter where the investigation took him.

IT WAS CHILDISH to blame her mother for dying. Only a foolish little girl would sit at the end of her mother's bed and curse under her breath at a woman who hadn't planned to drive in front of a truck with brake trouble. And Tara couldn't afford to be a foolish little girl anymore. She was the woman of the house now, or at least as much a woman as a girl of nearly eleven could be.

She was starting a new school this year, and Mama was supposed to go with her to sixth grade orientation. Daddy would be useless, grumbling his way through whatever presentation the teachers had planned, muttering things like "shouldn't be coddling young'uns this way" and "when I was this age, I was working in the fields all day, school or no school."

Now orientation was going to be horrible. And it was all Mama's fault for going away.

She pushed off her mama's bed and crossed to the window, looking out across their lawn at the house across the street. A new family was moving in, her father had told her. The Stiles family. Daddy had been in the Marine Corps with Captain Stiles, and he said the man was a good enough sort *for a gol dang officer.*

He hadn't actually said gol dang, but Mama had taught her she shouldn't cuss or use the Lord's name in vain, and even though she was really, really mad at Mama right now for going away just before sixth grade started, she still lived by Mama's rules.

A boy came out of the house across the road. A tall, skinny boy with dark hair that flopped across his forehead and braces on his teeth that glittered in the sunlight as he said something to his father as he passed.

The old man answered in a voice loud enough for Tara to hear it all the way across the road, though she couldn't make out the words. Whatever the man had said, it made the boy look down at his feet until the man had entered the front door with the boy he was carrying and closed the door behind him.

Then the boy's head came up and for a moment, Tara was certain he was looking straight at her.

She felt an odd twist in the center of her chest and stepped back from the window, not sure what she had just felt.

TARA WOKE SUDDENLY to darkness and a bone-biting cold that made her huddle closer to the warm body pressed close to her own. Owen, she thought, because of course it would be Owen.

It had always been Owen, ever since she'd first laid eyes on him the day of her mother's funeral.

The unchanging constant in her life.

He made a grumbling noise in his sleep, and his arm snaked around her body, spooning her closer. A humming sensation vibrated through her to her core, spreading heat and longing in equal measures. Oh, she thought, how easy it would be to let go and just allow this tension between them to build and swell to fruition.

She had a feeling it would be amazing, because Owen himself was amazing, a man of both strength and gentleness. She'd seen his passion—in his work, in his hobbies, and yes, even his passion for her, which flickered now and then like blue fire behind his eyes when he couldn't control it.

Keeping things platonic between them was difficult but necessary. Because Tara had lost enough in her life. She wasn't a coward, and she knew how to take calculated risks in order to achieve rewards.

But she could not lose Owen. She couldn't. Things between them had to remain constant or she didn't know what she would do.

Even when her body yearned for him, the way it was doing now. When it softened helplessly in response to the hardness of his erection pressing against the small of her back.

His hand moved slowly up her body, tracing the contours of her rib cage before settling against the swell of her breast. One fingertip found the tightening peak of her nipple through her T-shirt and flicked it lightly, making her moan in response.

Was he awake? His breathing sounded even, if quickened. Maybe he was seducing her in his sleep, giving sway to the urges they both kept so tightly reined in during their waking hours.

If he was asleep, it didn't really count, did it?

His fingers curled over the top of her breast, cupping her with gentle firmness. He caressed her slowly, robbing her of breath, before he slid his hand down her stomach. His fingers dipped beneath the waistband of her jeans and played across the point of her hip bones before moving farther down.

Closer. Closer.

He jerked his hand away suddenly, a gasp of air escaping his lips and stirring her hair. He rolled away from her, robbing her of his heat.

His breath was ragged now, ragged and uneven, a sure sign that he was no longer asleep.

"Tara?" he whispered.

She stayed still, her body still thrumming with hot need that would never be satisfied. That, she understood with aching sadness, was the cost of keeping her relationship with Owen the same as it had ever been.

But she could spare him the embarrassment of knowing she'd been awake for his dream seduction. Spare him knowing how very much she'd wanted him to keep touching her, to keep driving her closer and closer to the brink of ecstasy.

Behind her, Owen blew out a soft breath and sat up, being careful not to jostle her as he rose to his feet and headed outside the tent.

As soon as she was certain he was out of earshot, she rolled onto her back and stared up at the top of the tent, her heart still pounding wildly in her ears. She felt flushed and unsatisfied, and the urge to finish what Owen had started burned through her.

But she'd earned this frustration. She was the one who'd decided that it was too risky to test the sexual waters between them.

She would just have to live with the consequences.

Chapter Twelve

That had been close. Too close.

Owen let the water in the sink grow icy cold and splashed it on his face and neck, despite the chill bumps already scattered across his flesh from the walk through the woods this cold March morning. Another early riser, an older man brushing his teeth at the next sink over in the camp's communal men's room, glanced at Owen with curiosity but kept his comments to himself.

Owen could remember only a few tantalizing fragments from his dream, but the very real memory of Tara's hot flesh beneath his exploring fingers remained vibrant in his mind.

Thank God she'd still been asleep. Thank God he'd awakened before he'd allowed himself any further liberties with her.

He soaped up his hands and rinsed them, as if he could somehow wash away the sensation of her skin on his fingertips, but the feeling remained, on his skin and in his head.

He should feel ashamed. Dirty, even. But all he felt was a ravenous need to finish what he'd started in his dream.

He tried to gather his wits, get himself under control before he returned to the tent. But the man staring back at him in the mirror looked fevered and hungry, his blue eyes dark with the memory of touching Tara the way he'd longed to touch her forever.

He closed his eyes and bent his head, feeling tired. Tired of pretending he didn't feel what he most certainly did. Weary of denying himself the very natural desire he felt for Tara.

If he were going to be around her, he'd have to find a way to rein in that desire for good. He just didn't know if that was possible, which left one other option.

He could leave her life for good. Put her behind him, cut himself off from the constant temptation she posed and try to live without her.

As terrible as the idea of excising Tara from his life seemed to him right now, the thought of a lifetime of pretending he didn't want her as much as he loved her was even worse. It was a lie to behave as if he was okay with being nothing more than her friend.

He wasn't okay with it. He couldn't keep doing it.

The bearded man at the next sink had apparently watched the spectacle long enough. "Are you okay?" he asked.

Owen lifted his chin with determination. "I will be," he said.

He felt the other man's gaze follow him out of the bathroom. Outside, frigid air blasted him, reigniting a flood of goose bumps down his arms and back. Only belatedly did he realize that he shouldn't have drawn attention to himself the way he had. Even now his face might be plastered across TV screens throughout Kentucky and nearby states. How long before someone realized the scruffy-faced, bleary-eyed man in the hipster beanie they'd seen in the campground bathroom was the fugitive from Bagley County?

He didn't know whether to hope Tara was still asleep or awake when he got back to the tent, but when he ducked back into the tent to find her up and snugly dressed in a down jacket she'd bought back in Abingdon, he found he was relieved. The extra clothing she wore seemed like armor donned specifically to cool his ardor, which made him wonder if she'd been awake for at least part of his unconscious seduction.

But the smile she flashed his way was pleasant

and unclouded by any sort of doubt, so he decided she couldn't know what he'd almost done.

"I'm starving," she announced. "I was thinking, we should probably use up the eggs and bacon in the cooler, don't you think? Before the ice melts and they start to spoil? And I bought a little bottle of syrup back in Abingdon in case I got the chance to make my famous French toast. What do you think? French toast and fried bacon?"

He forced a smile. "Who could say no to French toast and bacon?"

"I'll go get the stuff from the cooler. Can you get the camp stove started?" She passed him in the opening of the tent, her arm brushing his. Even with the added layers of clothing they both wore, Owen could swear he felt the same tingle in the skin on his arm he'd felt in his fingertips when he woke that morning with his hand under her shirt.

He lowered his head until his chin hit his chest. How was he going to keep up appearances with her? Already, he was one raw nerve, acutely aware of her constant nearness.

It had to be because they were forced together by these circumstances, stuck in a situation where neither of them could go far from the other for any length of time. Back home, he could escape to his own apartment, indulge his fantasies about her and, on occasion, indulge his body's demands as well, without Tara having to know about any of those feelings or urges.

But there was nowhere to escape to now, no way to channel his desires without Tara knowing what was going on. He was stuck between the blissful heaven of being close to her and the burning hell of not being able to do a damn thing about it.

He forced himself out of the tent and went about the business of firing up the camp stove, glad for the distraction. But it lasted only as long as it took Tara to return from where they'd parked the SUV with the styrene cooler they'd picked up during their shopping trip. He felt her before he heard her footsteps crunching through the undergrowth. Her presence skittered up his spine like the phantom touch of fingers.

"I thought I'd bring the cooler to us so we didn't have to keep going back and forth to the SUV," she said as she set it beside him. "The ice has barely melted at all. I guess the cold snap helped slow the melting. I think we're good with the perishables for another day or so."

"Good," he said, mostly because he could think of no more cogent response. He backed away and let her take over at the camp stove, turning his back to the sight of her while pretending to take in the rain-washed beauty of the sunrise just visible through the trees to the east of them.

"I wish we'd thought to buy a radio," Tara said over the thumping of her spoon whipping the eggs into a batter. "I'd like to know what the news folks are saying about us after this weekend."

"Probably better not to know," Owen murmured. "I'm sure Quinn will keep us up with the latest news."

"I don't know," Tara muttered. "He's not exactly been a font of information to this point."

"He called when he said he would last night."

"And told us blasting nada."

He couldn't stop a smile. Tara had a thing about making up her own versions of profanities in order to avoid cursing. She'd told him once that her mother loathed swearing, even though she indulged her leatherneck husband's proclivity toward salty language. Tara didn't talk much about her mother at all, but he'd gotten the feeling that her attempts to temper her own language were a result of her mother's influence.

"Maybe there's nothing to tell yet," he said.

"It has to have hit the news by now, at least in Kentucky. Robert's family is very influential in Lexington."

"I'm sure it's been on the news."

"Which means whatever photos of us they

could find are being plastered all over local Kentucky news stations. And maybe Virginia ones as well, if they've figured out we were headed for here."

She was right. But what else could they do at this point? They'd already changed their appearances. His beard was growing in thick enough to change the way he looked, and the beanie and glasses made him even harder to recognize. Tara was almost unrecognizable with her new spiky haircut and ever-changing streaks of spray-on color in her hair.

He knew a few ways to go completely off the grid. Change their names, assume new identities with documents that would pass all but the most in-depth scrutiny. But that would be the act of someone who'd lost all hope of justice prevailing.

Had they really reached that point?

"Maybe we should have turned ourselves in to that Virginia state policeman I almost ran into back at the rest area," he said.

"They'd just send us back to the Bagley County Sheriff's Department and we'd be right back where we started." Tara rubbed her eyes, smearing the remains of her heavy mascara and eyeliner.

Without thought, he reached across the narrow

space between them and ran his thumb under her right eye to wipe away the worst of the smears.

Instantly, heat flared between them, searing in its intensity.

She trembled beneath his touch, her eyes darkening with unmistakable signs of desire. He'd seen such a reaction in her before but never this strong, this undeniable.

And in that instant, he knew. "You were awake."

She licked her lips. "Yes."

"Why didn't you stop me? Why didn't you wake me up?"

She looked away, closing her eyes. "Because I didn't want you to stop."

He touched her again, tipping her chin up to make her look at him. Her eyes fluttered open and again he was struck by the potency of desire he read in her gaze. "Tara…"

She drew away from him, shaking her head. "We can't, Owen. You know why we can't."

"Because you're afraid that it'll all go wrong and you'll lose me."

"I can't deal with losing you, Owen."

"Do you know what I was thinking about this morning? When I went to the restroom?"

She stared back at him mutely, the desire in her eyes replaced by apprehension.

"I was thinking that if things between us

didn't change, I was going to leave Kentucky. Go to Texas or California or, hell, I don't know, maybe Idaho. Anywhere you weren't, so I could get you out of my system once and for all. Because I don't think I can live in this endless limbo, Tara. Maybe you're okay with our relationship staying as innocent and platonic as it was when we met in sixth grade. But I'm not."

She stared at him in horror. "You don't mean that."

"I do, Tara. I'm sorry. I know you want to keep things the way they are, but people change. Circumstances change. I love you. Desperately. In every way a person can love another person."

"I love you, too."

"Then you have to let me go."

She shook her head violently. "No." She rose to her knees, reaching across the space between them to cup his face between her palms. "I don't want to let you go. I can't. You're all I have anymore."

He saw her expression shift, as if she finally realized what she was asking of him and why. Her eyes narrowed with dismay, and she looked so stricken that he wanted nothing more than to put his arms around her and promise her everything would be okay.

But he couldn't do that anymore. He'd finally reached his breaking point.

He put his hands on hers, gently removing them from his face. "I can't be your safety net, Tara. I don't want to do it anymore. If you can't take a chance on us, then that's fine. I'll accept it and go so we can both finally move on."

Tears welled in her eyes, but she blinked them away, anger beginning to drive away the hurt he'd seen in her expression before. "You promised you'd never let me down."

"I know." He hadn't let go of her hands, he realized, as if holding them was as natural as breathing. He gave them a light squeeze before letting go. "I just don't believe the status quo is good for either of us anymore."

Anger blazed in her eyes now, giving off green sparks. "Is this an ultimatum? Sleep with me or I won't be your friend anymore?"

"That is totally unfair, Tara! You know that's not what I'm talking about here." He turned away from her, anger beginning to overtake his own pain.

"That's the only thing we don't have between us, don't you see?" She caught his arm, tugging him back around to look at her. "We have everything else. Friendship. Understanding. Loyalty."

"We don't have marriage together. Children together. We won't make a family together or grow old together. If you think you can find a man or I can find a woman who'll put up with what we do have together, you're wrong."

"Robert was going to."

"Tara, Robert was already trying to push me out of your lives."

She stared at him, shocked. "No, he wasn't."

"Not where you could see it, no."

She sat back on her heels. "Why didn't you tell me?"

"I didn't want to come between you that way."

"If I'd known what he was doing, there wouldn't have been an us to come between," she said fervently. "Robert knew what you are to me. I made it clear from the beginning. One of the reasons I thought we could work together was that he took your presence in my life so well."

"Please, don't do this." Owen sighed, hating himself for even bringing up Robert's issues with him. "I don't want you to remember him badly."

"My life is so upended right now and I honestly can't understand why." She raked her fingers through her spiky hair, looking faintly surprised to find it so short. "I mean, intellectually, I can understand that someone wants to get his hands on something I know, and I also get that it's information that's dangerous for someone with bad intentions to know. But like I said earlier, I'm sure what I know has already been changed by my company. I'm as out of the loop now as anyone else."

"Is there anything you knew that could still be dangerous if someone else knew it?" he asked, glad for the change of subject. Despite his declaration to Tara about cutting the cord between them, he wasn't any more eager to do so than she was.

"I honestly don't think so. Whoever's taking over my job now that I'm gone is probably far more in danger for what he or she knows than I am now."

Owen frowned. "You think your bosses would already have put someone in your position?"

"I'm sure they have. It's not a job that can go unfilled for long, especially with the upcoming symposium details having to be changed so close to the planned time of the event."

So there was now someone else who knew the details of the symposium, Owen thought. Who was in the job only because Tara was now unavailable.

"What would happen if you went back to Mercerville and managed to get yourself cleared of Robert's murder?" he asked. "Would you get your job back?"

"If my bosses were satisfied that all the charges

against me were bogus, I'd say yes. We had a good relationship and I was good at the job."

"Even if they'd already replaced you?"

"I think so. It would be hard for someone to come in and learn my job in a few weeks, much less a few days. What I did, nobody else in the company duplicated."

"So how did they find someone to replace you?"

She seemed to give it some thought. "I guess they would have promoted my main assistant, although he wouldn't be able to pick up everything I was doing very quickly. It was a pretty complex system, with lots of security protocols in place. Plus, I had a more personal relationship with the people we were inviting to the symposium than anyone else in my section would have. That kind of interpersonal connection can be hard to maintain. Lots of personalities and egos involved."

Owen nodded. "Who is your primary assistant?"

"Chris Miller."

Owen pulled out his phone and typed in a text to Quinn.

"What are you doing?" Tara asked.

"Telling Quinn to do a deep background check on Chris Miller."

"You think Chris is involved in this mess?"

"I don't know," Owen admitted. "But we have to look at all the angles. Maybe the real reason Robert was killed was to make sure you couldn't go back to your job before the symposium began."

"Because I would be a suspect."

"We couldn't figure out why they kidnapped you. Maybe that's why."

"I thought they wanted to get the information out of me."

"Which would have been far messier than just making sure you were a suspect in a murder and unsuitable for classified work."

Tara cocked her head. "So by staying out here on the run, we're actually playing into the hands of the people who kidnapped me and maybe even killed Robert?"

"Maybe we are."

"So why is your boss making sure we stay where we are?"

That, Owen thought, was a good question. Alexander Quinn had a way of positioning his own allies as pawns in a bigger game. He would do everything possible to protect them, but sometimes collateral damage happened. An unfortunate but inescapable result of the high-stakes game Quinn and the people at Campbell Cove Security played.

"I guess maybe he's already figured out what's going on," Tara murmured, her eyes narrowed with thought. "Maybe Chris Miller is already on Quinn's radar."

Owen wouldn't be surprised if that were true. "But if he is, can he move fast enough to stop whatever plot is underfoot?"

"I don't know. It all depends on whether they moved the symposium back or up."

"What do you think they did?" Owen asked. "If you could read the minds of your company officers?"

"Up," she said after a moment more of thought. "If they moved the symposium up rather than back, it wouldn't leave bad actors much time to put their plot together."

"All the more reason to keep you on the run. Even if you went back now, you'd have to work through all the red tape and the explanations of why you fled in the first place. You wouldn't have time to get back to your job before the symposium took place."

Tara's lips twisted with irritation. "Damn."

Owen lifted his eyebrows at her curse.

One side of her mouth curled up in amusement at his reaction. "Sorry, but sometimes a profanity is the only word that'll do."

"So, what do you think we should do next?" he asked.

Her green-eyed gaze lifted to meet his, full of determination. "I think it's time to go home."

Chapter Thirteen

"So Ty Miller works evenings?" Archer Trask peered through his windshield, sunlight glaring off the back windshield of the vehicle in front of him. The rain that had soaked the area the previous night was long gone, replaced by blinding sunlight and rising temperatures.

"That's right," the receptionist on the other end of the line replied.

Ahead of him, the light turned green and traffic started to move. Trask put his phone in the hands-free holder. "What about Friday evening? Was he working Friday?"

"Let me check the schedule." There was a brief pause, and then she answered, "No, he was off Friday and Saturday."

"Is he working tonight?"

"Yes. He's scheduled to work every night through Friday of this week."

Trask grimaced. "Okay, thank you." He ended

the call and stared at the road ahead, frustrated. So far, his brother's alibi seemed to be holding, although Trask hadn't gotten far. For one thing, he didn't want Virgil to know what he was doing, because his brother would certainly want to know why he was trying to establish his alibi.

And for another, he wasn't sure he should be giving any credence to the story Heller had told him in the first place. It was a secondhand, maybe even thirdhand story from a pair of people who were currently on the run from the law. Some people, including his boss the sheriff, might not appreciate him spending time trying to prove his brother's innocence when there was an actual murder case on his plate.

The problem was, Trask was pretty sure Robert Mallory's murder was connected to whatever had happened to Tara Bentley the day of her wedding. He no longer thought she'd willingly left the church. But that left a lot of possibilities open, possibilities that didn't necessarily involve kidnapping.

Maybe Owen Stiles had spirited her away, not willing to watch her marry another man. Everyone seemed certain they were just friends, but Archer knew it was hard to keep sex out of the equation, friends or not. Tara Bentley was a healthy, attractive woman, and Owen Stiles was a healthy, reasonably good-looking man. The situation was ripe for sexual tension.

Had Stiles killed Mallory? Of the two fugitives, he seemed the more likely suspect. Jealousy, possessiveness, lust, obsession—all potential motives for murder.

But if he'd murdered Tara's fiancé, why was she still with Stiles? Was her friendship stronger than her love for and loyalty to the man she planned to marry? Or had she been the one whose feelings transcended friendship?

He rubbed his head as he reached the intersection with Old Cumberland Highway. If he turned left, he'd be heading back toward Mercerville and the sheriff's department, where three days' worth of paperwork awaited him. If he turned right, he'd end up in Cumberland, not far from Kingdom Come State Park.

He wondered if anyone in the area remembered seeing his brother and Ty Miller at the camping area outside the park the previous Friday.

When the light turned green and traffic started to move again, Trask signaled a right-hand turn.

"ARE YOU GOING TO tell Quinn what we're doing?" Tara looked up from stashing the last of the supplies in the duffel and stretched her back. "Because I don't think he's going to be happy that we're changing the plan he's working, whatever it is."

"Too bad. It's not his life. It's ours." With his usual precision, Owen folded the tent into a tidy square. He crossed to where she stood and slipped it inside the duffel before zipping it shut.

He stood close enough that she caught a whiff of the soap he'd used earlier when they risked heading into the more crowded camping area to use the campground's shower facilities. Not for the first time, she'd spent her shower time trying not to think of Owen naked under the spray of his own shower, water sluicing down his chest to catch briefly in the narrow line of hair that bisected his abdomen before dipping farther south.

But her imagination had seemed so much more potent, so much harder to deny, now that she'd actually felt his fingers against her flesh, moving with sexy determination, making her shiver with need.

Was this how it was for him, too? This trembling ache in her core when she looked at him, the way even his voice could send little flutters of awareness up and down her spine?

She was beginning to understand why he'd snapped earlier this morning. Wanting something you knew you could never have was painful. The pain didn't go away just because you were the one putting up all the obstacles, as she was coming to understand. Was it even worse when you were the person who wanted all the obstacles to disappear?

She had to clear her throat before she spoke. "It's probably better if we don't give him any forewarning."

"You do realize he knows exactly where we are, don't you?" Owen met her troubled gaze. "All of the Campbell Cove Security vehicles have GPS trackers on them."

"Even his personal vehicle?"

"Even his personal vehicle. While we were in the general camping area, I logged on to my computer and went through one of my back doors at the company to check the GPS monitoring. There we were, one stationary red dot on the map."

"So when we start heading back to Kentucky—"

"Quinn will know," Owen finished for her. He picked up the duffel and took a quick look around the campsite area to make sure they hadn't forgotten anything. They'd already packed all the other supplies, including the camp stove, into the back of the SUV. "But we should have a few hours of travel before he starts getting suspicious. Should we be planning our next moves during that time?"

"Probably should be," Tara agreed as she followed him through the undergrowth to the rocky path where the SUV was parked. "Except I'm not sure I know what those next moves should be."

"You don't think the first thing we should do is turn ourselves in?" He put the duffel in the back of the SUV and turned to look at Tara. "Isn't that the best way to get you reinstated at Security Solutions?"

"Theoretically, yes. But what if it doesn't work? What if we're locked away and nobody believes us? We need proof of our theory, and the only way to get that is to—"

"Don't say it."

"We have to break in to my office."

Owen shook his head. "Your office, which has probably had security doubled or tripled over the past few days? That office?"

"Yes. You're right, they've almost certainly hardened the security, but they're trying to keep terrorists out, not me."

"I'm not so sure about that."

"Okay, I guess it's possible they're trying to keep me out, as well. But either way, they're not trying to keep *you* out."

"Tara, I don't know anything about your company's security measures."

"You don't know yet. But you've spent the past few years as a white hat hacker, haven't you?"

"That's not what I call it."

"But it's what you are, right?" He gave a slight nod, and she pushed ahead, the idea making more sense the longer it percolated in her head. "With my knowledge of the company and its general protocols, and your knowledge of computer systems, I'm betting we can get inside the office building without being detected. Even at code red security, only certain areas of the building will be under twenty-four-hour surveillance."

"It seems to me that any part of the company where we might be able to discover anything helpful would be one of those areas of the building." Owen nodded toward the driver's door. "You want to drive or do you want me to?"

"You drove all the way here. I'll drive back. Maybe you could catch up on some sleep."

He looked skeptical as he climbed into the passenger seat.

While he buckled in, she addressed his previous protest. "You're right that the parts of the building where the most top secret material is kept will be under constant surveillance. But my office isn't one of those spaces. I went to the classified material when I needed it. I didn't take it out of its place of safekeeping."

"So your office won't be considered a high security risk area."

"Exactly."

"If that's so, how does getting into that area help us?"

"Because Chris Miller and I shared office space. Not right on top of each other, but in the same section. If I'm able to successfully get into my office undetected, I may be able to get into his office and see if there's anything incriminating to find."

"Do you expect there to be?" Owen asked curiously.

She considered the question carefully. "Honestly, I don't know. The only thing about Chris Miller that's ever given me pause is that he's a little too friendly."

Owen frowned at her. "Friendly how?"

She glanced at Owen. "Not that kind of friendly. I just mean, he doesn't have a suspicious bone in his body, which is weird for a guy who works in security. I've had to warn him about phishing emails, that kind of thing. He opened an email not too long ago and nearly let loose a virus in our system. I figured out what he'd done just in time to warn our IT guys and they stopped the program before it could open up any holes in our cybersecurity."

"How does he even keep his job? For that matter, why on earth would he be next in line for your job?"

She made a face. "Nepotism. Chris's uncle is the founder of our firm."

"Maybe he's the weak spot in your company's security without even knowing it," Owen suggested. "Someone could be using him. Manipulating him to get the information they want."

"More likely than not," she agreed. "Which is why I need to get into the office and see what he's been up to. It might help me find out if anyone has been trying to exploit his position to get secure information."

Owen remained silent for a long time while they headed southwest on I-81 to Abingdon. Only as they exited the interstate and began heading due west toward Kentucky did he speak again. "You realize if we get caught, it will make it nearly impossible to prove our innocence."

"I know. But it may be our only chance to find out what's really going on and who's behind it in time to stop whatever they're planning. That's reason enough to take the risk, don't you think?"

As Tara braked at a traffic light, Owen reached across the space between them and touched her face with the back of his hand. "Has anyone ever told you what a brave person you are?"

She stared back at him, a shiver running through her at his touch. For a moment, as their gazes locked and the air in the SUV's cab grew warm and thick, she found herself wondering if she'd made the wrong choice all those years ago when she felt the tug of attraction to Owen and ruthlessly subdued it. What if he was right? What if they could have everything? Their deep and enduring friendship and the heady promise of intense passion?

Wasn't that what everyone really wanted? To have it all?

The traffic light changed to green. Owen dropped his hand away from her cheek and nodded for her to drive on.

She headed west on Porterfield Highway, feeling chilled and unsettled.

WORKING FOR A small law enforcement agency had its benefits and its drawbacks. For the most part, Archer Trask liked the slower pace of his job at the Bagley County Sheriff's Department. There was enough petty crime to keep him busy most of the time, and in such a small place, he generally got to know the citizens he helped as people rather than impersonal names and case file numbers, the way he had done when he worked a couple of years in the Louisville Police Department before returning home to Bagley County.

But one of the drawbacks of working for a small agency was the glacial pace at which the wheels of information gathering turned. Which was why it had taken almost a day for a simple background information request about the security company where Ty Miller worked to make its way to his email inbox.

He had just spent a frustrating hour trying to track down anyone in the Cumberland area who might have seen his brother and Ty Miller up near Looney Creek on Friday, but the problem was, Kingdom Come State Park wouldn't open until the first of April, and most of the people who weren't park visitors had been too busy at their own places of work on Friday to notice if a couple of middle-aged men had wandered by with fly rods and tackle boxes that day.

In fact, he had begun to think he'd wasted a whole day chasing a false lead when his phone pinged with the email notification. He pulled over onto the shoulder and checked the message. It was from Don Robbins, the deputy he'd assigned to dig up background information on Cumberland Security Staffing.

He read through the list of companies that hired the staffing company to provide security personnel for their firms. There were a couple of shopping strip centers, a movie theater, a couple of mining companies and even a church or two that had showed up on the list of clients.

It was only on his second read through that Trask came across a familiar but unexpected name.

He stared at the email for a moment, then dialed a phone number, unease wriggling in his stomach as he waited for an answer.

"Security Solutions," answered the female receptionist.

"This is Deputy Archer Trask. Is this Diane?"

"Yes, Deputy," she said, her tone warming as if she were pleased that he'd remembered her name. "How can I help you?"

"Diane, does your company still use Cumberland Security Staffing?"

There was a brief pause before she replied, "I'm not really supposed to answer that question."

"Could you put me through to someone who can?"

There was another pause. "I've been asked not to disturb any of the officers this afternoon." She lowered her voice. "Is it urgent for you to know this information right now?"

"Yes," he answered. It was urgent to him, at least.

"We do employ them. They provide our four night guards."

"Can you tell me the names of the guards?"

"I don't know if I can do that—"

"Okay, maybe you can tell me this. Is one of them named Ty Miller?"

After a long pause, Diane whispered, "Yes."

"Thank you, Diane. You've been very helpful."

He hung up the phone and stared at the narrow road stretching into the mountains ahead of him. So Ty Miller was a security guard at Security Solutions, the company where Tara Bentley worked. And according to Maddox Heller, Tara Bentley was kidnapped by two men outside the church where she was supposed to marry Robert Mallory, who had mysteriously turned up murdered in the groom's room.

Tara Bentley, who had told her lawyer that his brother Virgil was one of the men who'd kidnapped her.

His brother, Virgil, whose alibi for the day of Robert Mallory's murder and Tara Bentley's alleged kidnapping was Ty Miller. Who worked for the same company as Tara Bentley, albeit indirectly.

Trask rubbed his temples, his head aching with the sudden twists and turns his murder case had started to take. Worse than the complications was the fact that he didn't know what he was supposed to do next. Bring his brother, the deputy investigator, in for questioning? Interrogate Ty Miller about his whereabouts on

Friday, even though he had less probable cause to question him than he had where Virgil was concerned?

He needed to find Tara Bentley and Owen Stiles. They were the only people who really knew, firsthand, what had happened to them the day of Robert Mallory's murder.

"WHY ARE YOU back in Kentucky?" Quinn's voice was tight with annoyance over the cell phone speaker.

Owen glanced toward Tara. She gave a nod. "Tell him."

"How secure is this line?" Owen asked Quinn.

"About as secure as any cell phone can get. Someone would have to be listening for your transmissions specifically to find you. Or get very lucky."

"I'm not sure that's secure enough."

"Then perhaps we should meet," Quinn said.

"Where?"

"Where Maddox picked you up Saturday," Quinn answered. It was oblique enough a response that only Owen, Tara, Maddox Heller and Quinn would know where he meant.

"I can do that," Owen said. "In about an hour?"

"I'll see you there." Quinn hung up.

Tara glanced at Owen. "Do you think he'll try to talk us out of it?"

Owen thought about the question for a moment, then shook his head. "No. I think he'll devise some ingenious way for us to get away with it."

For the first time in many miles, Tara shook off her troubled expression and managed a smile. "I think maybe I'm starting to like Alexander Quinn."

"Don't go crazy, now," Owen joked, to cover his own anxieties starting to rise to the surface the closer they got to Bagley County. He wasn't as sure as Tara that breaking into her company office was a smart thing to do. The risks were high and the possibility of rewards was scanty in comparison.

Maybe he'd been right that Quinn would support their crazy scheme, but he wasn't sure he'd consider that good news.

Chapter Fourteen

So far, Ty Miller hadn't answered any of Trask's calls, and attempts to catch him at home had so far proved futile. However, a check with the receptionist at Cumberland Security Staffing had revealed that Miller would be working the night shift at Security Solutions tonight, starting at eleven.

In the meantime, Trask had been studying his file on Robert Mallory, trying to examine the case from a different angle. Mallory's death had seemed to be the main event, with Tara Bentley's disappearance a side story. But what if that assumption was wrong? What if Tara's disappearance were the focus of the crime, with Mallory's murder a peripheral event?

Had Mallory stumbled onto something that had led to his murder? Could he even have been complicit in whatever had led to his fiancée's kidnapping?

"Assuming she was kidnapped," he muttered as he checked the clock on his office wall. Only a little after five. Almost five more hours to go before he could head to the Security Solutions compound and wait to catch Ty Miller before he started work.

With a sigh, he returned his attention to the files. He preferred legwork to paperwork, but at least this particular bit of paperwork involved trying to pull together the scattered threads of a mystery.

Starting with Tara Bentley.

Who was Tara Jane Bentley? He knew the basics—the only daughter of former Gunnery Sergeant Dale Bentley and Susan Bentley, both now deceased. She was born in Campbell Cove, grew up there and only left town to attend the University of Virginia.

Trask paused, reaching for a second stack of papers. Hmm. Owen Stiles had also attended the University of Virginia. Coincidence? Unlikely.

He set aside questions of their unusually close friendship, since it would only lead him back to mundane motives for Robert Mallory's murder, and that road hadn't been leading him anywhere definitive.

For the past five years, Tara had worked at Security Solutions, a nonprofit think tank dedicated entirely to analyzing security threats both global and domestic and searching out strategies for prevention and even prediction of future events, helping security experts to stay ahead of the terrorist threat rather than reacting after an event took place.

Since joining as an analyst, she'd moved quickly up the company ladder to director of global relations, whatever that meant. Because the company was a nonprofit entity, she wasn't exactly rolling in dough, though his tiptoe through the company's public profile suggested she made a decent salary.

But he'd already examined the idea of a profit motive in Robert Mallory's murder, at least where Tara Bentley was concerned. Mallory's income had been generous, and would've grown considerably as he took over more and more of his father's law practice. He'd recently become a partner, and if Tara Bentley had gone through with marrying Mallory, she could have led a financially comfortable life indeed. But she wasn't going to see a penny of his money now, since he'd died before the wedding.

So what had really happened the day of the wedding that had left Mallory dead and Tara Bentley running for her life?

Could it have anything to do with his brother Virgil and his elusive alibi for the day in question?

Trask leaned back in his chair and rubbed his burning eyes, feeling further from the truth than ever.

"WE ALMOST WENT to this school," Tara commented as Alexander Quinn walked with her and Owen down the long corridors of Campbell Cove Security. "It closed about two years before our freshman year. Do you remember?"

"Vaguely," Owen said, looking around. "I guess I never really gave any thought to what this place was before it became Campbell Cove Security."

"It was scheduled to be demolished before I came in and bought up the property and the building." Quinn's tone was brisk, as if he was annoyed by the trip down memory lane.

Tara kept her mouth shut for the rest of the walk. When they reached the end of the corridor, instead of turning right or left, Quinn led them forward through a dark red door marked Exit.

Outside, twilight had fallen while they were in Quinn's office, updating him on everything they'd done since their last contact. Tara had been expecting a little more pushback from Quinn about their breaking-and-entering plan, but he'd been remarkably positive about the idea, with a couple of caveats.

"First, if something goes wrong, there can be no direct links back to my company," he said firmly. "So that means I can't send you any of my agents to help you out with your plan. Just Owen, and he's not going to be there in any company-related capacity."

"Understood," Tara said quickly.

"And second, if you do end up in trouble because of this, I'm not going to be able to help you the way I have so far. You'll be on your own completely. Can you deal with that?"

Despite the tightening sensation in the pit of her gut, Tara had nodded.

"We have to figure out what's really going on before we risk going to the police again," Owen added with more resolve than Tara felt. "There could be a terror plot already in motion, and this could be our chance to stop it cold."

"Which is exactly why I'm going along with this crazy plan," Quinn said with a smile. "And why I'm going to help you figure out all the angles so we can avoid any of the obvious pitfalls."

Among the obvious pitfalls, Tara had learned, were the exact security protocols followed by Security Solutions' night security team. Quinn refused to reveal just how he'd come by the information, but he was able to tell them when the security patrols would be in what part of the building. "It's not smart to stick to a set plan," he'd commented with disapproval, "but I guess that's the price of outsourcing your site security instead of building your own in-house staff."

Tara's guess about the company's security focus had been correct. Except for a single walk-through of the company's nonsecure office wing early in the shift, just after eleven o'clock, the security patrols would spend the rest of their eight-hour shift patrolling the secure areas. None of the guards had keys to the securest rooms, where the classified material was, Quinn told them. "You won't be able to get in there, either," he warned.

"We don't think we'll need to," Tara assured him.

Over the next couple of hours, they'd worked out a plan that even Quinn agreed might get them in and out of the building without detection. He admitted he'd already checked with Tara's bosses to see if they'd done anything about revoking her credentials. They hadn't, they'd admitted. They weren't ready to give up on her innocence, and blocking her credentials seemed too much like admitting she could have done something wrong.

"Foolish sentimentality" had been Quinn's succinct assessment, but at last it made it more likely she could get through inside her office building without triggering any alarms.

"They'll have evidence of an ingress," Quinn warned, "and they'll have the code number used to enter, if they decided to check the security system logs."

"If I don't trigger an alarm, they won't have any reason to check," Tara told him. "And even if they do, all they'll see is that someone entered the office building using the security code for my department. But everyone in the department uses the same code number to disarm the alarm."

Quinn's stony expression was as good as an eye roll. "Our nation's security is in good hands."

"Well, it'll work in our favor this time," Owen murmured.

They'd shared a pizza with Quinn while going over a quick checklist of things they wanted to accomplish and how they planned to go about it. There was a brief discussion about using night vision equipment to aid in their getting safely inside the security perimeter, but they all agreed that since both Tara and Owen lacked experience with night vision equipment, the goggles would be more of a detriment than an asset.

Finally, Quinn had handed over a couple of heavy backpacks and led them down the corridor to this exit into the encroaching woods behind Campbell Cove Security.

"We're being banished to the woods?" Tara

murmured as she struggled to keep up with Owen's long strides behind Quinn.

"I have no idea," Owen admitted.

Ahead of them, Quinn strode confidently through the dark woods, avoiding obstacles in the underbrush as if he knew exactly where they were, even though the path beneath their feet was little more than a tangle of weeds and vines, anything but well traveled.

About a hundred yards into the thickening woods, they reached a small clearing of sorts. There were no trees in the small area, but kudzu vines took up the slack, nearly covering what looked like a small shack in the middle of the woods.

"It used to be one of the school's outbuildings," Quinn told them as they approached the kudzu-swallowed building. Only the door remained vine free, and even it would have been difficult to pick out at a cursory glance, painted with a mottled green camouflage pattern that nearly perfectly matched the surrounding kudzu. "We left the kudzu when we cleaned it up and put it to use. Cheaper than camo netting."

Inside, the place was remarkably clean. It was little more than a room with a couple of camp beds, a tiny kitchen area with a sink, a one-burner electric cooktop and a mini refrigerator. The door in the back of the building led to a small but usable half bath with a tiny shower and an even tinier sink.

"Please tell me this works," Tara said as she eyed the shower with near desperation.

"It all works. Electricity and plumbing should get you by until you have to leave for your rendezvous with Security Solutions," Quinn said. "I had someone park the SUV in the woods due north of here, just off the road into Mercerville. They've topped off your fuel tank and changed out the license plates again, just in case." He slanted them a wry look. "Got rid of the bumper stickers, too."

"Thought of everything," Tara murmured.

"You'll stay here until then. I thought you might both enjoy a hot shower and a hot meal. From this point forward, I expect no contact from either of you unless you achieve your ends. Agreed?"

Tara glanced at Owen. He gave a brief nod.

"Agreed," Tara said. Owen echoed her response.

"Clean up after yourselves and try not to knock off any of the kudzu." Quinn opened the door, quickly slipped out and closed it behind him.

The silence that fell afterward made Tara feel as if she were about to smother. The small outbuilding itself wasn't cold, nor was it overly warm, but it felt closed in, suddenly, after days of living outside or in an SUV.

"I'll be magnanimous and give you first dibs on the shower," Owen said. He had taken a seat on one of the camp beds and was digging through the backpack Quinn had supplied. He pulled out each piece and laid it on the bed, revealing a couple of changes of clothes, a pair of hiking boots and a handful of protein bars. Owen waved one of the protein bars at Tara as she sat on the bed opposite. "He meant what he said about cutting us loose, but at least he gave us a change of clothes and a couple of meals to get us through to the next hidey-hole."

"Yay?" Tara pulled out the clothes Quinn had provided for her. They looked as if they'd fit well enough, though she longed for her own closet and her own wardrobe.

What she wouldn't give to be in her cute little house in Mercerville, cuddled up in front of the fireplace.

With Owen, an unrepentant little voice whispered in her ear.

She grabbed the change of clothes and headed for the small bathroom. "I'll try not to use up all the hot water."

Easy enough, she thought as she turned the cold tap all the way on.

ARCHER TRASK EYED the clock as he closed up the file folders. Three hours to go, and he wasn't any closer to a theory about Robert Mallory's murder than he'd been when he started.

Unless he wanted to believe his brother and Ty Miller really had kidnapped Tara Bentley and killed her fiancé.

But what was the motive? Trask's brother was a pretty ordinary guy. Divorced, no kids, worked a tough job and spent his off time hunting, fishing and four-wheeling. About the average for a guy from Bagley County, Kentucky. He wasn't particularly religious or political, as far as Trask knew, which would seem to rule out those particular motives.

As far as Trask knew. Which was the problem, wasn't it? Even when they were younger, he and Virgil had never been close. Virgil was a decade older than Trask, and he'd never had much time for his younger half brother, too busy raising hell with his friends to do any brotherly things with his tagalong sibling.

After a while, Trask had stopped trying to be close to Virgil, which had seemed to be fine with him.

There was quite a lot about Virgil that he didn't know, wasn't there?

Really, if anyone knew Virgil at all, it was their father, Asa. He had always had a soft spot for Virgil, even during the worst of his delin-quency. *We used to call it sowin' wild oats*, Asa would say when Trask's mother complained about Virgil's latest misdemeanor.

Trask had long suspected that Asa had never really gotten over his first wife. Marrying Trask's mother, Lena, had been a matter of ex-pediency—he had a young boy who needed a mama, and he was a man who needed a warm body in his bed. Lena Lawrence had been a beauty in her youth, and she'd fallen hard for the older widower with a child.

Trask suspected she'd long ago given up on true love and was still married to the old man much for the same reason he'd married her in the first place—neither of them wanted to go through life alone.

He picked up his phone and dialed his parents' number. His mother answered, her voice warm, "Archer, how are you?"

With some embarrassment, he realized it had been at least two weeks since he talked to his mother. "I'm good," he said quickly, realizing she might be wondering if he was calling with bad news.

Of course, in a way he might be.

"I heard you're workin' that murder case at the church."

"Yeah. I can't really talk about it."

"Oh, I know. Your daddy's always tryin' to get Virgil to spill the beans about his cases, too, but Virgil tells him just enough to make him want to know more, then laughs and says it's police business and he can't spill the beans." Even though there was laughter in his mother's voice, Trask could tell she didn't like Virgil's form of teasing. "Makes your daddy crazy."

"Speaking of Virgil, have you seen much of him lately?"

"Some, here and there. He's been spendin' a lot of time with Ty Miller. You remember Ty, don't you?"

"Yeah, I remember Ty. What are they doing, hunting and fishing?"

"No, they just seem to hang out in Ty's garage with some of their friends, smokin' and talkin' if he's not on duty."

"Really?" That didn't sound much like Virgil, who'd never been much of a joiner. "Who's he hanging out with besides Ty?"

"Oh, I don't know. I think I saw one of the Hanks boys there a couple of weeks ago, and Chad Gordon. Jenny Pruitt mentioned to me at church Sunday that her boy, Dawson, was hanging out with Ty, too." His mother's voice darkened. "She sounded a little worried about it, to tell the truth."

"Why's that?"

"I don't rightly know. I told your daddy about it, but he said not to worry, Virgil's a deputy now and we don't have to mind his business anymore." Lena laughed. "Thank goodness for that. He was a handful."

"I suppose we both were."

"Oh, you had your moments," Lena said, "but I never had to worry about bailing you out of jail in the middle of the night. Listen, I know it's a little late, but I'm betting you're calling from work, aren't you? I have some leftover supper— we had fried chicken, green beans and mashed potatoes. Your favorite. You want to drop by on your way home?"

"That's real tempting," Trask said, meaning it. "But I've got to work for a few hours longer tonight. But I'll definitely take you up on the offer the next time you cook my favorites."

"Oh, okay, then."

The disappointment in her voice almost made him give up on his idea of confronting Ty Miller at work tonight. What would it really accomplish? So far, even the accusation against Virgil was third hand. He had yet to speak to Tara or Owen Stiles, face-to-face or otherwise. Hell, the only reason Ty Miller was on his radar at all was that Virgil had unwittingly named him as his alibi.

But Archer needed to hear that alibi himself,

read Ty Miller's face and decide whether or not he was lying for Virgil.

"I'm really sorry," he told his mother. "I'll drop by and see you just as soon as I get a minute of free time."

"I'll look forward to it," she said, her tone loving. He felt an ache of love for his mother throbbing deep in his chest. He didn't know if she was living the life she wanted, but she was the sort of person who made do with what she had and looked for the bright side of every situation.

She deserved a more thoughtful son than he had been lately.

"Love you, Mama. I'll talk to you soon."

"I love you, too, sweet boy. You be careful, all right?"

"Will do." He hung up the phone, his eyes going toward the clock.

A little after nine. Almost showtime.

THE COLD SHOWER had done nothing to calm the urgent throb of heat at her core or the itchy, unsettled feeling that she was walking into the heart of danger with so many important things left unspoken.

If they were right that Robert's murder was about keeping Tara on the run, then they might encounter someone armed and very dangerous at her office tonight. She, Owen and Quinn had

gone to great lengths to tie up all the loose ends
and make tonight's break-in go as smoothly and
safely as possible, but even Quinn had acknowl-
edged the risk.

She had no family to say goodbye to. Her
friends were mostly people Robert had known
or a handful of women she'd gone to high school
or college with and rarely talked to anymore now
that their lives had gone in different directions.

Owen was her family, her circle of friends,
her rock. And she had denied him the only thing
he'd asked of her in all the years of their friendship.

He was a man. They were attracted to each
other. She was asking a lot of him to deny those
feelings while continuing to be her friend.

But she couldn't bear life without him. He was
her true north.

The heat in her core spread up into her belly
and breasts, sending a quiver down her spine
as the door to the small bathroom opened and
Owen stepped out, wearing only a pair of jeans
and a towel around his neck. His hair was still
damp from the shower, a trickle of water sliding down his chest to follow the dark line of hair
that dipped beneath the waistband of his jeans.

Friends with benefits. Wasn't that what people
called it these days? She knew there were other
terms for it, vulgar terms, but what she felt with

Owen wasn't vulgar or base. She loved him. She just wasn't ever going to risk being *in* love with him. That complicated everything beyond hope.

But being his best friend, who he happened to sleep with now and then—that was something she could handle, wasn't it?

Owen gave her an odd look as he swiped the towel down his chest a couple of times before he tossed it aside and met her in the middle of the small room. "Is something wrong?"

She nodded, trying to find her voice. But her mouth was dry and her heart was pounding, drowning out all her thoughts.

"What is it?" Owen asked, his voice dropping to a gravelly half whisper.

"I was wrong," she said, her own voice coming out raspy. "I was wrong about us."

His brow furrowed, but he waited for her to speak.

Instead of words, she chose action, rising to her tiptoes and curling her fingers through his damp hair. She moved closer, sliding her other hand up his chest, reveling in the crisp sensation of his chest hair beneath her palm.

Owen opened his mouth as if to speak, but she didn't let him get that far. With a sharp tug of her hand, she pulled his head down and covered his mouth with hers.

Chapter Fifteen

She tasted like honey and heat, her lips soft and her tongue insistent, parting Owen's lips and demanding entry. He was powerless against her, just as he'd always known he would be. Tara was his soft spot, his Achilles' heel. In the end, he could never deny her anything, and that was why he was still by her side, long after a sane man would have walked away to find greener pastures. Tara was his one and only, and for all his talk of walking away, he now understood he never would do so.

Her hands seemed to be everywhere—on his shoulders, his sides, the tips of his fingers and the skin just above his hip bones. He was on fire, an unquenchable heat that seemed to grow and spread wherever she touched him.

Finally, her fingers dipped to the zipper of his jeans, and while every inch of his flesh seemed to sing with joy, a mean little voice in the back of his head asked a question.

What is she really offering you?

As if she'd heard the sudden note of discord, Tara stilled her hand and pulled back to look at him, her eyes dark with desire. "What's the matter?"

He wanted to tell her nothing was wrong, to proceed with what she'd been doing. Everything would work out the way it was supposed to.

But he'd never been a guy who worried about the future when the future came. He was the guy who had his week planned on a spreadsheet. He was that much like Tara, he supposed, or maybe all these years of friendship had made her control freak side rub off on him.

He had to know what she was really offering before he agreed to take it. For better or for worse.

"What are we doing here?" he asked softly.

She gave him a quirky half grin. "Been that long?"

"Been forever, but that doesn't really answer my question."

Her fingers fluttered lightly against his rib cage, sending shivers down his spine. "I'm seducing you."

"I thought you were against our pursuing a romantic relationship."

A small frown creased her forehead. "I'm not against a sexual relationship. I think we could handle that, don't you? Solves the sexual tension problem, but we don't muck up our friendship with other kinds of expectations."

His heart sinking, he pulled her hands away from his body. "Sweetheart, that won't solve anything."

"Why not? People do this all the time. Friends with benefits."

"That never ends well."

"We could make it end well." She rose to her tiptoes to kiss him again.

And he let her. Drank in the sweetness he found there, the passion and the promise of pleasure. Drank and drank, losing his will to resist. Maybe this could work, he told himself as he wrapped his arms around her waist and dragged her closer, flattening himself against her so he could feel all the soft curves and strong edges of her body. He had known her intimately for years, except for this part of her, the seductress with a wicked imagination and an unimaginably sweet touch.

But what happens when she's ready to start a relationship with someone else again? the mean little voice asked.

With a low growl of frustration and regret, he pushed her away.

"No, Owen, don't do this…"

"I have to," he said, sinking onto the edge of the nearest bed. "Someone has to be sensible about this."

"No, don't you see? We've been too sensible about this for too long. We should have known we could figure out a way to have what we both want. We always have." She sat beside him on the bed, too close. The scent of bath gel on her heated skin was intoxicating.

He caught her hands before she touched him again. "I don't want sex from you, Tara."

She looked confused. "But isn't that the problem?"

"No, sweetheart, it's not. Sex is just a part of what I really want."

Her eyes flickered with annoyance, so very Tara-like. She hated when someone contradicted one of her plans. And nine times out of ten, if he was the one thwarting her will, he'd have gone along with her just to see her beautiful smile when she got her way.

But this was too important a decision to give in to Tara just to see her smile. Their friendship was on the line. One way or another, something had to give, because he couldn't bear to be just her bed buddy and her best friend.

He wanted what she'd been so ready to offer Robert Mallory, even though Owen had known all along she'd never loved Robert enough to spend forever with him. He knew it because he knew, deep down, that he and Tara were supposed to be together.

But what he knew, or thought he knew, didn't matter at all if Tara didn't see it, too.

"I don't want to be your best friend forever or your friend with benefits, because that will never be what you are to me." She started to speak, but he touched her lips with his fingertip, stilling them. "Tara, I love you. I have loved you since the time you pantsed Jason Stillwell for stealing my lunch money. That love has never faltered, even through your snotty cheerleader years and the time you decided that dating only frat boys at Virginia was the best way to reach your life goals."

She grimaced. "Don't remind me," she said against his fingertip. He dropped his hand and she flashed another quirky half smile at him. "I love you, too, Owen. You know that."

"I do. But do you love me enough to marry me?"

Her expression froze, and for a moment, she turned so pale that he thought she was going to pass out. But then her color came back, rising to fill her cheeks as if she'd pinched them.

"Marry you?"

"Yes. Rings, cake, children, forever and ever and ever."

"No. I can't marry you." She pulled away from him, pacing across the floor to stand near the kudzu-draped front window. She stared into the greenery, clearly seeing something else. "You know why I can't."

"Just because your parents' marriage was a mess doesn't mean yours will be. You were willing to marry Robert."

"Because he ticked off everything on my list," she said, her voice rising with distress. "It felt like a sign. This is the one."

"But he wasn't."

Her face fell. "No, he wasn't."

"Because I am."

She didn't look at him. Didn't speak.

With a sigh, Owen retrieved his watch from the small bench beside the table and checked the time. Getting close to eleven. In an hour, they should be just outside the Security Solutions compound, sneaking in through a small back gate that most employees knew nothing about. Even Tara hadn't realized the gate existed until Quinn showed her where to look on the property.

"We'll have to table this for now," he said. "Let's get dressed and packed up. We have a long walk to the SUV. If we wait too long after the guards do their check on the office buildings, we won't have as much time to look for evidence before we have to leave."

She turned away from the window, her expression composed. She walked past him to the other bed and sat on the edge to pull on a pair of thick socks. "Dress warmly," she said. "Judging by the air I felt coming through that window sash, it's getting really cold out."

He pulled on a long-sleeved black T-shirt and shrugged a thick black sweater over it. The jacket Quinn had supplied was also black, a medium-weight Windbreaker that should keep him warm enough as long as the clouds scudding overhead didn't start spitting out snow rather than rain.

The hike to the SUV was painstakingly slow in the dark, and the heavy silence that had fallen between him and Tara didn't help to make the forward slog any more enjoyable. He finally spotted the SUV's gleam through the trees about a hundred yards ahead and breathed a sigh of relief.

He handed over the SUV keys to Tara. "Your company. You drive."

She took them without a word or even a smile and climbed behind the steering wheel. He rounded the vehicle and got in the passenger seat, looking at Tara's grim profile as he buckled up. "I don't think we can accomplish this mission without talking to each other."

"I'm sorry. I just don't know what to say."

He shook his head. "There's nothing else to say about us, is there? You're not willing to risk our friendship for something more, and I've come to the conclusion tonight that I can't walk away from you, even if I know deep down it's what I should do. So we go on the way we always have."

She looked at him. "Can we?"

"I don't know what else we can do. Do you?"

She shook her head and faced front again. For a moment she didn't move at all, just sat still and silent, her gaze fixed on something outside the SUV. Then she released a soft breath and put the key in the ignition. The SUV's engine roared to life.

Moving forward in the deepening night, they fell back into silence again.

THERE. JUST WHEN Archer Trask was beginning to think the receptionist from the security staffing company was wrong, Ty Miller's black pickup truck turned into the driveway of the Security Solutions compound and parked near the gate.

Trask was reaching for his door handle when he realized that Miller wasn't alone.

Easing his hand away from the latch, Trask leaned over to open his glove compartment and retrieve the small set of binoculars he kept there.

He lifted the lenses to his eyes and took a closer look at the passenger seat of Miller's truck.

His stomach twisted as he recognized his brother's craggy face.

Damn it, Virgil.

THERE WAS NO good place to park the SUV, but Tara pulled the vehicle as far off the road as she could, hoping the darkness and the trees that lined the access road would be enough to hide the vehicle from any curious eyes that might pass by at this late hour.

The only real perimeter to the Security Solutions compound was an aging chain-link fence about eight feet high. Razor wire twists had been added at some point in the recent past, but there wasn't any real security outside of the kiosk just inside the front gate, and even it wasn't manned after hours. Employees had a key card that would allow them to enter through the automated gate, and anyone else would have to wait until morning for the daytime crew to arrive.

Getting in without going through the front gate, however, would seem to require a climb over the tall fence and braving the vicious edges of the razor wire. But somehow Alexander Quinn had uncovered a utility gate near the back of the property that made it possible for public utility repairmen and also law enforcement to enter the property after hours if necessary. It was a convenience not known to many in the company, Tara was certain, because she'd never heard a thing about it, and she was placed fairly high in the company's hierarchy.

"I'd guess he learned of it from your bosses themselves," Owen opined when she remarked on Quinn's knowledge of the back gate. "Or maybe from some of his law enforcement contacts. Quinn always seems to know where to find information he needs and how to exploit it."

"You make him sound scary."

"Most of the time he is."

They located the gate after a frustrating search through overgrown weeds and grass outside the company grounds. A heavy chain had been looped through the gate latch, giving the outward look of a locked gate, but closer examination revealed there was no lock at the end of the chain. All they had to do was unwind the chain to open the gate and enter.

"Now what?" Owen asked.

"We're about three hundred yards from the building, I'd estimate." Tara peered through the gloom, trying to get a sense of perspective. "There's a side entrance on the east wing of the building, where my office is located. It opens with a key card, but if for some reason you can't put your hands on a key card, it'll also open with a numerical code."

"Not very secure."

"Well, after the third time Clayton Garvey left his key card at home and had to go through the humiliation of fetching a guard to let him in, they changed the system."

"You'd think people who deal in security threats would be able to identify the ones in their own systems."

"Human nature." They were close enough now to see the building looming in the darkness like a sleeping steel-and-glass behemoth. "That's the door we're heading for."

They slowed down as they neared the entrance, taking care not to draw attention to themselves. Just because the security guards would now be focusing attention on the more secure parts of the building didn't mean she and Owen didn't have to take precautions as they entered and started moving around. There were cameras at the end of each corridor, and while these weren't controlled by motion sensors, she and Owen would still need to be quick in hopes of avoiding immediate detection.

The cameras record everything, which is why you need to wear the masks I've provided until you're out of range of the corridor cameras, Quinn had warned them. They stopped now, while still clear of the building's external security cameras, to slip on the knit masks Quinn had put in their backpacks.

"Ready?" Owen asked, making last-minute adjustments to his mask.

"Yes."

He motioned for her to lead the way.

UNTIL THE VERY last moment, Trask had planned to confront his brother before Virgil and Ty Miller ever set foot into the building. But then Virgil had stepped out of the truck wearing the same security company uniform that Ty wore, and Trask was suddenly uncertain about everything he'd believed he knew.

As he froze in place, his mind racing through all the possible implications, Ty and Virgil walked across the narrow space between the parking lot and the front entrance, disappearing inside the building.

The automatic gate was still slowly closing. Spurred into action, Trask jumped from his truck and raced through the gate with inches to spare. But when he tried the front door, he found it locked.

He hadn't noticed Virgil or Ty stop to punch in an alarm code after entering, so he might be able to pick the lock without setting off any sort of alarm.

Within a few moments, he felt the last of the pins in the lock open and he gave the door a tug. It swung silently outward and he slipped into the building.

Stopping to listen, he didn't immediately hear any other noises. Wherever Ty and Virgil had gone, they'd gone quickly. There was an elevator bank a few feet inside the foyer. Maybe they'd taken the elevator to another level?

He moved toward the bank of elevators, glad he'd worn soft-soled shoes. They made a tiny, almost imperceptible squeak on the polished floors, but at least he wasn't leaving echoing footsteps ringing behind him as he walked.

He looked at the elevator indicator lights. Hmm. All of them seemed to read Ground Floor. Wherever Ty and Virgil had gone, it appeared they hadn't gone by elevator.

Wandering a little deeper into the building, he spotted his first security camera. It stood still, which might mean it was showing a static image on a security monitor somewhere. If so, his presence here would need some explaining. Somehow he didn't think his bosses at the sheriff's department would be satisfied with whatever he managed to come up with.

Too late to worry about that now. He backtracked until he found an office directory sign. There were two wings, it appeared. The one he was in was called Administrative Services and included a long list of offices and names. Tara Bentley's office was on this floor, he saw, in an area marked Analytical Security Services Unit.

He had no idea what that meant, he realized. Or what, really, Tara did for Security Solutions. It was all very vague in general, the way a lot of job descriptions at security companies could be.

Owen Stiles's position at Campbell Cove Security was only slightly less mysterious, and that was only because Trask had a better grip on what "cybersecurity" meant than "analytical security services."

Maybe this was his chance to find out a little more about who his mysterious fugitive bride really was.

He turned right and headed for Tara Bentley's office.

Chapter Sixteen

The corridors were mostly dark, except for a few lights near the tops of the walls that shone at half strength every ten yards or so. Tara kept an eye on the security cameras as she walked quickly up the hall. She and a couple of her coworkers had noticed that just before each camera made a sweep of the service area, it twitched twice in the opposite direction of its eventual sweep. Then it would move in a slow arc before going stationary again until its next sweep.

The one down the hall started to twitch twice to the left. Tara grabbed Owen's arm and pulled him through the nearest door.

"Is this it?" Owen whispered.

"No, it's a conference room."

"Then why did we come in here?"

She told him about the camera sweep observation.

"How long will the sweep last?" Owen asked.

"Should be over now." She risked a quick peek into the hall and saw the camera sitting still again. She grabbed Owen's hand and they hurried up the hall, pausing as they reached a corner.

She took a quick look around the corner. It was empty, and the camera at the end of the hall was still. "Let's go."

Owen followed her forward as she led him swiftly down the corridor and around another corner. They managed to reach the door to her office without the cameras moving again.

But to her surprise, the door to her office was locked.

"These doors aren't usually locked," she whispered, giving the knob a second, futile twist.

"Let me take a look. You keep an eye on the cameras."

"Move in as close to the door as you can. I don't think the camera's view reaches into this alcove." Tara flattened her back against the door and watched with curiosity as Owen pulled a small leather wallet from his pocket. He unfolded the flaps to reveal a series of narrow metal rods of various sizes, all small. It was a lock-picking kit, she realized with surprise as Owen selected two of the metal pieces from the wallet and tucked the rest of them back in his pocket.

He inserted both pieces into the lock, wiggled them around in ways that made no sense to her whatsoever. But within a couple of minutes, the door lock gave a slight click and Owen twisted the knob open.

He entered first, with caution. Tara followed closely behind him, her hand flattened against his spine. "My desk is over here on the right. Chris Miller's desk is here to the left."

Suddenly, the light came on in the room, almost blinding her with its unexpected intensity. She squinted, wondering if Owen had flicked on the light. She was about to tell him to turn the lights off again when he stopped dead still in front of her, his back rigidly straight.

She realized with a sinking heart that he hadn't been the one who'd turned on the lights.

A drawling voice greeted them, a twist of humor tinting his words. "Well. This is an unexpected turn of events."

She turned around to see the man who'd lured her out to the church parking lot standing in front of them, holding a big black pistol.

"Hey!"

The voice that rang through the corridor behind him stopped Trask short. He turned slowly to find himself looking at Ty Miller, no longer dressed in his drab olive security uniform but a pair of khaki pants and a dark blue blazer over a white golf shirt.

No, that wasn't right. This man was younger, though his hair color, his features, even his general build were the same as Ty Miller's. In the low lighting of the nighttime building, it had been easy to see what Trask was expecting to see.

He hadn't been expecting to see Ty's brother Chris, even though he was also an employee of Security Solutions. It was after midnight now. What the hell was he doing here at this hour?

"Archer," Chris said as he stepped closer. "What are you doing here?"

"Looking for your brother, actually."

Chris looked puzzled. "Is he working tonight? He told me he was off this week. Guess he must be covering someone else's shift."

"What are you doing here this late?"

"I have an analytical paper to present tomorrow to the officers about the sym—" Chris bit off the last word. "For something we're planning. Anyway, I realized I left some files here in my office that I need to return to the secure section before morning, so I came here to get it."

"Do you mind if I come with you? This place is a little creepy at night. Don't tell my boss I said that."

Chris grinned. "It's our secret. And you're right. It's creepy as hell."

They headed down a long corridor side by side. The oppressive silence continued to make Trask's skin crawl. Then, suddenly, he heard the quiet murmur of voices coming from somewhere down the hallway and faltered to a halt. Chris Miller stopped short, too, an odd expression on his face.

When Chris spoke, it was in a whisper. "Nobody's supposed to be in this wing at this hour. Security should already be on the other side of the complex."

Trask eased his hand beneath his jacket and closed his fingers over the butt of his service pistol. He kept his voice as low as Chris's. "One quick question. Did you know my brother was working security here these days?"

Chris gave Trask an odd look. "No, he's not."

"Maybe he just started."

"No." Chris's voice rose a notch. He tamped it back down to a hiss of breath. "If we'd hired new security people, I'd know. One of my jobs is to screen the personnel Security Staffing sends our way. I'd know."

Damn it. Trask swallowed the bile rising in his throat and nodded toward the continuing murmur of voices drifting up the hallway. "Let's go find out who's here."

"Ty, GET OUT HERE." The man in the drab olive uniform kept the muzzle of his pistol pointed directly at Owen's heart. Owen forced his gaze away from the muzzle and concentrated on taking in every detail of their captor's appearance.

Definitely the same man he'd seen trying to shove Tara into the panel van outside the church. Also definitely the same man who'd been entering the Bagley County Sheriff's Department in a deputy's uniform the morning they tried to turn themselves in.

"You're Virgil Trask," Tara said, her voice strong, though Owen heard the slightest tremble on the last word.

"And you're a real pain in the ass, lady. Not real good at stayin' put."

"What were you planning to do with me? What was the point of drugging me and dragging me away from the church?"

Virgil looked at her as if she'd lost her mind. "Do you think this is some sort of *Scooby Doo* episode? You think I'm going to stand here and waste time telling you all the details of my nefarious plot?"

"You can't just shove us out of here at gunpoint," Owen said. "Security cameras will catch it all."

Virgil shot him a withering look. "Who the hell do you think runs the security cameras around here?" He turned his head toward a door in the back of the room. "Ty, you comin' out here or not?"

A big broad-shouldered man emerged from the door, his arms full of files. "He left them here, just like he said, Virgil." The man Virgil Trask called Ty stumbled to a stop, dropping a couple of the file folders stacked in his arms as he spotted Owen and Tara. He muttered a soft profanity.

"Yeah," Virgil said with a grimace. "I was really hoping I wouldn't have to kill anyone just yet."

"Do it now, do it later," Owen said with a studied shrug. "It's what you have planned, isn't it? Killing a whole lot of people from a whole lot of countries who are wanting to clamp down on terror attacks across the globe? What I don't understand is why."

Virgil said nothing, but Ty Miller dropped the rest of the folders he held onto a desk nearby and took a belligerent step toward Owen. "You think those people are coming here to make us all safer? They're just looking at more ways to tie our hands behind our backs."

Virgil shot Ty a look of disgust. "Would you shut up, Ty? Let's just figure out a clean way to get rid of them and get back to what we're here for."

"Those files are from the classified section," Tara said, taking a few steps toward the files Ty had just deposited. "Chris had them in his office?"

"Uncle Stephen let him take them out for some paper he's preparing to present to the directors. You know Chris, he doesn't get everything on the first read through."

Tara glanced at Owen, looking faintly horrified. "And he left them in his office?"

"Stop talking, Ty. I mean it." For a moment, Virgil's pistol swung toward his partner in crime. It was a tiny opening at best, but Owen had a feeling there wouldn't be another.

He launched himself toward Virgil, knocking him hard into the nearest desk. Virgil hit it with a loud grunt of pain, already swinging his pistol back around toward Owen.

But Owen had already jerked the backpack from his shoulders and held it in front of him, using it to shove the pistol wide as Virgil pulled the trigger. Big puffs of fabric and insulation flew from the backpack as both Owen and Virgil fell to the floor.

"Owen!" Tara screamed.

All the breath seemed to rush from Owen's lungs, and the world around him started to go black.

THE SOUND OF a gunshot was easy to mistake for other things. A vehicle backfiring, or even the crack of a baseball bat hitting a pitched ball.

But neither of those things could be found inside this building at nearly half past midnight. While Chris Miller froze in place, Trask's cop instincts sent him running toward the sound.

A woman's voice rose in a wail. "Owen!"

The sounds seemed to be coming from the office just down the hallway, the one marked Analytical Security Services Unit. Trask would bet what little money remained in his savings account that the woman's voice he just heard belonged to Tara Bentley.

He'd found his fugitives. He just hoped it wasn't too late.

As TARA STARTED across the room to where Owen had fallen, Ty Miller grabbed her arms and held her in place. She struggled against his hold, but he was as strong as a bull and his grip was already digging deep bruises in her flesh.

Still, she kept fighting, her heart racing with terror as she watched Owen go dreadfully still.

"Let me go!" She kicked back against Miller's legs, her boot apparently connecting with one of his kneecaps, for he let out a howl of pain and his grip on her arms loosened.

She tore out of his grasp and ran to Owen's side.

"Get back!" Virgil trained his pistol on her from his position on the floor, desperation tinting his deep voice. "Get back, or I'll shoot you, too."

She lifted her hands toward him. "Please, let me go to him."

Virgil shook his head. "Stay where you are."

"He's hurt!" She could see a dark, wet patch spreading on the side of Owen's jacket. "I have to stop the bleeding or he could die."

"He's going to die one way or another." Virgil nodded toward Ty, who grabbed Tara's arms and pulled her backward again.

"We need those files, Virgil," Ty said.

"I'll get them. You take the girl."

"What about him?" Ty asked.

Virgil looked down at Owen. "He'll bleed out sooner or later. Then we'll come back here to clean up."

Tara thought for a moment she saw Owen's hand twitch, but after that he was completely still, and she guessed with despair that she'd seen only what she wanted to see.

He might already be dead, his heart stopped by

Virgil Trask's bullet. He could be gone and there were so many things she still hadn't told him.

Like how much she loved him. How much the image of that forever love he'd talked about had burrowed its way into her soul that she understood now how impossible it would ever be to walk away from what he was offering.

Now, when it was too late, she finally got it.

Don't die on me, Stiles. Don't die on me before we have our shot at forever.

CHRIS MILLER HAD remained where he stood down the hall while Trask made his way to the closed door. Just as well, he'd probably be more of an obstacle than an aid.

Trask waited against the wall, trying to hear what was being said inside the room. He heard the low rumble of his brother's voice, and the broader country drawl of Ty Miller answering. They were talking about cleaning up after themselves. Something about files. The woman was begging them to let her go to someone. She'd cried out Owen's name, so maybe Stiles had taken that bullet he'd heard fired down the hall?

"Let me go!" Tara's voice rose again to a shriek.

"Get her out of here!" Virgil bellowed.

Trask flattened himself against the wall, waving down the hall for Chris Miller to get out of the way.

Chris scurried down the hall and rounded the corner, out of sight. Trask saw him reaching for his phone as he ran. Calling 9-1-1? Trask hoped so.

There was a hard thud against the door, followed by several more thumps.

Then splinters of wood flew from the door beside his head in concert with another blast of gunfire. Trask ducked, his heart galloping in his chest.

"WHAT THE HELL, VIRGIL! You nearly hit me." Ty Miller released one of Tara's arms, giving her the chance to pull away. Her cheek stung where a splinter of wood from the gunshot had sliced through the skin, but she didn't think she'd been hit anywhere else.

She jerked free of Ty's grasp and turned to look at Virgil. But he wasn't standing there holding a gun as she expected. Instead, he was grappling on the floor with Owen, whose eyes were open and locked with Virgil's. His hand covered Virgil's on the pistol, and he shouted, "Get out of here, Tara!" without ever looking in her direction.

He was alive. The words sang through her whole body, sending a flood of sheer relief pouring through her like fizzy champagne bubbles. But reality crashed through the brief moment of jubilation. He was still wrapped in a death grip with a man who'd already shot him once. And another man was already moving toward them, ready to help his buddy overpower Owen.

She grabbed the chair that sat near the door and swung it at Ty Miller, catching the big man right in the small of his back. Something made a loud cracking noise, and it wasn't the solid steel chair she'd somehow managed to wield like a club. Ty howled with pain as he crashed to the floor, writhing in agony.

"Go, Tara! Go!" Owen shouted as he started to lose his grip on Virgil's arm.

"No!" she cried, picking up the chair again and heading to his rescue.

Ty Miller's hand clamped around her ankle, stopping her short. Losing her balance, she fell hard to the floor, the impact sending stars sparking through her brain for a moment. She pushed through the disorientation and kicked with her free leg, hitting Ty in the chin. He yelled out a stream of profanities but let go of her leg.

She scrambled up again and grabbed the chair, grunting as the full weight of the steel behemoth made itself known. Earlier, with adrenaline spiking her strength, it had felt almost featherlight, but the adrenaline was starting to drain away.

She gazed desperately at Owen, who had managed to grapple Virgil Trask toward the window.

Suddenly, the door behind her slammed open, and both Virgil and Owen froze to look at the newcomer. Tara turned as well and found herself looking at a dark-haired man holding a big gunmetal-gray pistol. He aimed the pistol's muzzle across the room at Virgil Trask.

"Put the gun down, Virgil. It's over."

Owen let go of Virgil and stumbled back, falling into a chair a few feet away. Tara ran to him, her heart in her throat.

"What are you doin' here, Archie?" The tone of Virgil's plaintive query was somewhere between anger and dismay.

"I'm here to put an end to all of this, Virgil. Put down the gun."

Virgil shook his head. "You don't know what this is, Archie. I caught your fugitives. He tried to kill me."

"That's a lie!" Tara shouted as she paused in the act of trying to find the source of the blood dripping on the floor beneath Owen. "These two men tried to kidnap me the day of my wedding. I think one of them killed my fiancé. They're after some secret information."

"I know," the man in the doorway said. "I'm Archer Trask. I'm the lead investigator on your fiancé's murder case."

"Come on, Archie! She's your top suspect, and I found her. I was going to bring her in."

"It's over. Just put down the gun."

"Archie, it's me."

Archer Trask stared at his brother sadly. "I know, Virgil."

Suddenly, Virgil's gun hand whipped up a couple of inches, and Tara shouted a warning.

It wasn't necessary. Gunfire blazed from Archer Trask's pistol at the same time Virgil pulled the trigger of his own weapon. The bullet Virgil fired went wide, hitting the doorframe behind his brother's head. His brother's bullet, however, hit Virgil in the chest.

For a minute, Virgil stared in disbelief at the bloom of red spreading across his shirt. Then he looked back at his brother, the stunned expression frozen on his face as he slid to the floor. His chin fell to his chest, and only the desk beside him and the wall behind him, now streaked with his blood, kept him from falling over.

Archer Trask walked slowly to his brother's side, gazing down at him with a look of pure grief. He nudged the pistol away from his brother's slack fingers with his toe, moving it out of reach. Then he crouched in front of Virgil and touched his fingertips to his brother's throat.

The look of sheer agony on his face told Tara what that trembling touch had revealed.

Archer sat back on his heels, tears leaking from his eyes. "Damn it, Virgil," he said.

Chapter Seventeen

"Do we have to do this now?" Tara looked at the grim face of Bagley County Sheriff Roy Atkins as he loomed over where she sat in one of the small interrogation rooms at the county hall complex. "I know Deputy Trask must have already told you everything that happened tonight. I just want to make sure Owen is okay."

"He's still in surgery."

Shock hit her like a fist blow. "Surgery? He's in surgery? Why is he in surgery? He was awake and talking, and the paramedics seemed to think he was okay—"

"He was shot in the side. They want to be sure he didn't sustain any life-threatening internal injuries, so they need to get the bullet out of him before it causes any worse problems."

"Surgery?" She pressed her hand to her mouth, terror twisting her insides. She had thought it was over. She just had to get through all the debriefings, convince the authorities that she had been running for her life, and then she and Owen could move forward with the life they should already have been living together.

This couldn't be happening. Not now.

Owen deserved the forever he wanted so desperately, and somehow she had to find a way to give it to him.

But she couldn't do it from here, halfway across the county from where he lay on an operating table, fighting for his life.

A brisk duo of knocks on the door drew Sheriff Atkins's gaze in that direction. His look of mild irritation deepened when Tony Giattina walked confidently through the door and set his gleaming leather briefcase on the table between the sheriff and Tara.

"Don't say anything else, Tara," he said, looking at her with far more sympathy in his expression than had been there the last time she saw him. He was dressed in an expensive-looking suit and a crisp linen shirt that would have been more at home at a morning court appearance than a two in the morning visit to the county jail. "Sheriff, are you planning on holding my client overnight?"

For a moment, the sheriff looked as if he wanted to say yes. But finally, he shook his head. "Just don't leave our jurisdiction this time, Ms. Bentley."

"She wouldn't dream of it," Tony said blithely, offering Tara his hand. She took it and rose, following him out of the interrogation room.

Outside, the corridor was buzzing with more movement than she'd noticed when she was first brought in. A lot had happened, including the death of one of their own deputies. That he'd been the cause of his own death hadn't really sunk in at this point, and some of the deputies sent furious glares her way as she walked out of the building with her lawyer.

To no one's surprise, Alexander Quinn was waiting outside the sheriff's department. He nodded toward Tony before turning his attention to Tara. "Are you all right?"

"I need to see Owen. The sheriff said he's in surgery."

"He is. One of my colleagues is there with him, waiting for word. I'm here to take you to the hospital." He opened the passenger door of a dark blue SUV and helped her inside. As she buckled in, he climbed behind the wheel and reached for his own belt. "On the way, why don't you tell me everything that happened tonight?"

One way or another, she thought with resignation, she was going to have to undergo an interrogation after all.

THE LAST PEOPLE Archer Trask had expected to see sitting at the bar of the Sheffield Tavern were Maddox Heller and his pretty wife. He almost turned around and walked out when he saw the expressions of sympathy in their faces, but he braced himself against the unwanted kindness and walked over to where they sat.

The bar was nearly empty at this time of the morning. It would close in another hour, which would at least give him a polite reason to escape, he thought with bleak humor.

"We heard what happened," Heller said as Trask settled on the bar stool next to him. "I'm sorry."

"So am I," Trask said. He waved at the bartender. "Bourbon and branch. Light on the branch."

"We think we've finally figured out what your brother and Ty Miller were involved in," Heller said. He had a glass of what looked like water with a twist of lime and had drunk a little of it. Even the wife was nursing her glass of white wine, barely taking a sip at all as she looked from her husband's face to Trask's.

"I can guess at some of it," Trask said. "My mother told me Virgil had been spending a lot of time with Ty Miller and some of his friends. I had a chance to talk to Ty's brother, Chris, for a few minutes before the police and emergency services arrived. He said Ty had gotten involved with some group of preppers."

"They weren't just preppers. Preppers mostly just want to be left alone to prepare for whatever might come," Heller said. "Your brother and his friends were determined to make sure our country cut its ties with the rest of the world. Extreme isolationism, I guess you could call it."

Trask remembered a few of the more objectionable things he'd heard his brother say over the years. He could definitely see him falling on the side of "kick the foreign bastards out and don't let them back in."

"Quinn and his previous security company back in the mountains of Tennessee came across a very similar group of nihilists—the Blue Ridge Infantry. We think one of the men in this group of people had familial ties to some of the former members of the Blue Ridge Infantry."

"I've heard of them. They were in Virginia, too, and there were less organized groups here in Kentucky with sympathetic leanings."

"I think maybe Ty and your brother were in the process of trying to organize this Kentucky group into something more cohesive. Through Chris, they found out Security Solutions was planning a security event that involves several other countries. I think your brother and Ty must have realized that if they could create a big, deadly disruption of that event, their success would be a spectacular recruiting tool to pull off bigger and more influential attacks against the government they think has betrayed them. But they needed more information about the event to be successful."

"So they kidnapped Tara Bentley? Why? To get her to tell them what she knew?" Trask asked with a frown. "You think they were going to try to torture it out of her?"

"We thought that might be the case at first," Heller admitted. "But we couldn't quite make Robert Mallory's murder fit our theory."

The bartender arrived with the bourbon and water. Trask took a sip and grimaced. "Neither could I. It seemed to be completely out of the blue. No motive seemed to fit."

"They wanted Tara Bentley out of the way, and they wanted the cops looking in a completely different direction," Heller said. "If they'd killed her, where would your investigation have taken you?"

"To her. Her connections. Her job," Trask answered. "But instead, it was her fiancé who died. And she was my prime person of interest instead of the victim. I didn't even look at her work as a possible reason for what happened until recently."

Heller nodded. "Your brother was a cop. He would have known the direction you'd look in."

"Leaving him and Ty free to look for the information they would never have gotten from Tara."

"They planned to stash her somewhere until they got what they wanted from her second-in-command."

"Ty's brother, Chris." Trask took another sip of the bourbon. It burned all the way down, leaving him feeling queasy and unsettled. He pushed the drink away. "They found some files tonight."

"We heard. Security Solutions has already sent people from their secure documents division to return them to a place of safekeeping."

"I don't think Chris was intentionally involved."

"We don't think so, either," Heller agreed. "He was just too careless for the job he was tasked to do."

Trask stood up, feeling stifled and claustrophobic in this place. He pulled a couple of bills from his wallet and put them on the bar next to his drink. "I gotta get out of here."

Heller and his wife followed him outside. "Trask," Heller said, stopping him in his tracks.

He turned to look at them. "I really need to be left alone."

It was the wife, Iris, who reached out and took his hand. As had happened the last time they met, he felt a strange zip of energy flow through him where her fingers touched his flesh. "I'm so sorry about your brother. If you need anything, you give us a call, okay?"

She flashed him a faint smile, removed her hand and walked away with her husband.

Trask turned to watch her go, rubbing his hand where she'd touched him. Just a moment ago, he'd felt as if he'd never feel normal again. But now...

Now he felt as if there just might be a sliver of hope out there after all.

"HE'S OUT OF SURGERY. He did just fine." A tall, beautiful African American woman rose as Quinn and Tara entered the surgical waiting room. "I tried to reach his parents, but I got no answer."

"I think they're in Branson, Missouri," Tara said. "They go there every spring, before the summer tourist rush kicks in." She rubbed her gritty eyes, surprised to find tears trembling on her eyelashes. "I want to see him."

"I know. They'll take him up to his room as soon as he's out of recovery." The woman offered Tara a gentle smile. "I'm Rebecca Cameron. I work with Quinn at Campbell Cove Security."

"Right. Owen's mentioned you."

Rebecca put her arm around Tara's shoulders. "Come on. I'll take you to his room."

The empty room looked so sterile. Tara found herself futilely wishing the hospital gift shop downstairs was open so she could at least buy a nice vase of spring flowers to make the place look more homey and welcoming.

As if she had read Tara's thoughts on her face, Rebecca patted Tara's back. "I suspect all he really needs right now is you." With an encouraging smile, Rebecca left her alone in the room.

It seemed to be forever later when a nurse and an attendant wheeled Owen into the hospital room on a gurney. He wasn't exactly awake, but his eyes were fluttering open and closed and his arms flailed weakly as he tried to help the attendant move him from the gurney to the bed.

The nurse finished settling Owen and put his IV bag on the pole beside him. She turned to smile at Tara. "Are you Tara?"

Tara nodded.

"He asked if you were here when he first started coming out of the anesthesia."

Tara crossed to Owen's bedside. His eyes were closed again, but when she took the hand without the IV, he squeezed weakly.

"Tara?" he mumbled.

"Right here, Owen. Where else would I be?"

The nurse smiled at her again. "I'll be back in a bit to check his vitals. You can stay in here with him if you want. I could get you a reclining chair if you like. To make it more comfortable."

"That's fine. Thanks. No hurry. Just when you can get to it." She waited until the nurse walked out the door, and then she bent closer to Owen. "You gave me a scare, you big, brave idiot. Don't ever do that again."

His eyes fluttered halfway open, though his pupils seemed incapable of focusing. "Admit it. You were impressed by my show of manly courage."

"Terrified is more like it," she confessed, her heart surging with relief to hear him making jokes. "I didn't need proof of your strength, you know. I've always thought you were the strongest man I know."

"No matter what my father thought?"

"By now, we both know he's a fool. So stop trying so hard to prove it, okay?" She touched his cheek. "For the dozen years you scared off my life span, you owe me big, mister."

His dry lips cracked into a lopsided, painful-looking smile. "Yeah? You got a payment in mind?"

She leaned even closer, lowering her voice to a whisper. "How about you marry me?"

His eyes struggled to focus. "Was that a proposition?"

"It was a proposal." She picked up the roll of

tape the nurse had left on the bedside table after she taped down his IV cannula. Stripping off a piece, she wrapped it around his left ring finger. "See? I got a ring and everything."

A raspy laugh escaped his throat. He winced, and when he spoke again, his voice was hoarse but full of humor. "Why, Miss Tara, this is so sudden."

"Say yes, Owen."

"Yes, Owen." His eyes fluttered shut.

She drew up the chair beside his bed and sat there with a goofy smile on her face, her fingers twined with his.

OWEN WOKE TO sunlight angling through a window, falling across his eyes and making his head hurt. He turned his head with a grumble and found himself face-to-face with Tara.

She was just starting to wake, her eyes fluttering open. She gave a slight start when she saw him watching her. Pulling back from the bed, she laughed sheepishly. "Good morning."

He winced in pain as he shifted position in the bed. "That's a matter of opinion."

"Are you in a lot of pain? Do you want me to call the nurse?"

"No, please don't. She kept waking me up all night."

Tara brushed his hair away from his face.

"Oh, come on, you slacker. You slept through the last couple of vitals checks. I was awake for all of them." She rubbed her red eyes. "God, I need about a week of sleep."

"How did you get the police to let you come here?" His throat felt as if he'd swallowed glass. Probably the breathing tube they'd have administered before surgery.

"Quinn sicced Tony Giattina on them. They didn't know what hit them."

"Tony's speaking to us after what we did to him?" He was surprised.

"Well, that's still up in the air." Tara touched his face, her expression gentle. "You look terrible."

"Thank you. You don't know how much better that makes me feel."

"I thought I'd lost you." Her fingers moved lightly over his forehead, her touch strangely tentative, as if she weren't sure whether she had a right to offer him comfort. "When I realized you'd been shot, I was so scared."

"I'm okay. Everything's okay." He put his hand over hers. As he did, he noticed a piece of tape wrapped around his left ring finger. A vague memory drifted through his brain. Tara holding his hand, talking about debts. But the rest of the memory eluded him, somehow distant and unreachable.

"I love you," she murmured, pressing her lips against his palm. "I was so afraid I'd never get to tell you that again."

"Oh, I already knew that." He gave a weak wave of his other hand, wincing a little as the IV cannula shifted in his vein. He was aching all over and felt as if he'd gone about ten rounds with a freight train, but a sense of peace began to settle over him. Everything was going to be okay now. His wound would heal and he and Tara would get their lives back.

"What are you smiling about?" Tara asked, rubbing her cheek against the back of his hand. He liked the feeling, liked the way it sent little flutters of life through his otherwise lifeless body.

"Just thinking that it's finally over. The truth will come out, one way or another, and we'll get to go back to our lives again."

"Do you remember anything about last night?"

"I remember running into Virgil and Ty. I remember getting shot. Then someone shot Virgil."

"Deputy Trask," she said, her voice darkening. "Virgil's younger brother."

Owen grimaced. "Poor bastard."

"What do you remember after that?"

"You holding my hand. Paramedics. Lots and

lots of lights, and then it's a blank." He narrowed his eyes at her. "Did I miss something?"

"Quite a bit," she said with a wry half smile.

"I remember seeing you after surgery," he added. "If that's what you're getting at."

"Yes, I was waiting for you when you came up after recovery."

"You told me I owed you big."

"That's right." Smiling, she ran her finger lightly over the edge of the tape on his finger. "I also told you the payment I wanted."

He looked at the tape on his finger, then back at her face. What he saw in her eyes made his heart turn a little flip in his chest. "Did I agree to your terms?" he asked, emotion swelling through him to settle like a lump in his throat.

Tears glittered in her eyes. "Yes, but you were a little loopy at the time."

"So maybe you should tell me again. What do I have to do to even up things between us?"

A smile crept over her lips. "Marry me, Owen Stiles. Make me your wife."

He caught her hand in his, pressing it against his chest. "Why, Tara?"

She frowned, as if she hadn't expected the question. "Because I love you."

"You loved me yesterday and the day before that. But you weren't anywhere near thinking about marrying me. Don't make a big decision just because we've gone through a crisis."

"I'm not. I was already thinking about it before you were shot. It's just, staring down the barrel of a gun really clarifies things for you, you know? I realized that I might not get the chance to tell you that the one thing I wanted more than anything in this world was to live the rest of my life with you. To be with you in every way. It suddenly seemed so stupid to be afraid of having everything with you. I trust you completely. With my life. And with my heart." She stroked his cheek, the tears spilling down her cheeks. "I know now that we belong together in every way. I believe that with all my heart."

He had trouble pushing words past the lump in his throat. "So ask me again."

Her eyes met his, deadly serious. "Will you marry me, Owen Stiles?"

"I do believe I will," he answered, pulling her down for a kiss.

* * * * *

Look for the continuation of Paula Graves's
CAMPBELL COVE ACADEMY *miniseries*
when OPERATION NANNY
goes on sale next month.

You'll find it wherever
Harlequin Intrigue books are sold!

LARGER-PRINT BOOKS!

HARLEQUIN

Presents®

PASSION
GUARANTEED
SEDUCTION

GET 2 FREE LARGER-PRINT NOVELS PLUS 2 FREE GIFTS!

LARGER-PRINT BOOKS!
GET 2 FREE LARGER-PRINT NOVELS PLUS
2 FREE GIFTS!

H HARLEQUIN®

super romance®

More Story...More Romance

WESTERN WP PROMISES

YES! Please send me **The Western Promises Collection** in Larger Print. This collection begins with 3 FREE books and 2 FREE gifts (gifts valued at approx. $14.00 retail) in the first shipment, along with the other first 4 books from the collection! If I do not cancel, I will receive 8 monthly shipments until I have the entire 51-book Western Promises collection. I will receive 2 or 3 FREE books in each shipment and I will pay just $4.99 US/ $5.89 CDN for each of the other four books in each shipment, plus $2.99 for shipping and handling per shipment. *If I decide to keep the entire collection, I'll have paid for only 32 books, because 19 books are FREE! I understand that accepting the 3 free books and gifts places me under no obligation to buy anything. I can always return a shipment and cancel at any time. My free books and gifts are mine to keep no matter what I decide.

272 HCN 3070 472 HCN 3070

Name	(PLEASE PRINT)	
Address		Apt. #
City	State/Prov.	Zip/Postal Code

Signature (if under 18, a parent or guardian must sign)

Mail to the **Reader Service:**

IN U.S.A.: P.O. Box 1867, Buffalo, NY 14240-1867
IN CANADA: P.O. Box 609, Fort Erie, Ontario L2A 5X3

WPBPA16R